UNDER THE
BRIGHT LIGHTS

A RINEHART SUSPENSE NOVEL

A RINEHART SUSPENSE NOVEL

UNDER THE BRIGHT LIGHTS

DANIEL WOODRELL

HENRY HOLT AND COMPANY
NEW YORK

Published by Henry Holt and Company, Inc.,
521 Fifth Avenue, New York, New York 10175.
Published simultaneously in Canada.

Library of Congress Cataloging-in-Publication Data
Woodrell, Daniel.
Under the bright lights.
(A Rinehart suspense novel)
I. Title.
PS3573.06263U5   1986   813'.54   85-27313
ISBN 0-03-008514-4

First Edition

Designed by Katy Riegel
Printed in the United States of America
1   3   5   7   9   10   8   6   4   2

ISBN 0-03-008514-4

To Katie, for all the reasons

You can map out a fight plan or a life plan, but when the action starts, it may not go the way you planned, and you're down to your reflexes — that means your [preparation]. That's where your roadwork shows. If you cheated on that in the dark of the morning, well, you're going to get found out now, under the bright lights.

—*Joe Frazier*

UNDER THE BRIGHT LIGHTS

A RINEHART SUSPENSE NOVEL

1

Jewel Cobb had long been a legendary killer in his midnight reveries and now he'd come to the big town to prove that his upright version knew the same techniques and was just as cold. He sat on the lumpy green couch tapping his feet in time with a guitar he scratched at with sullen incompetence.

It was hard to play music in this room, he felt. There was a roof but it leaked, and great rusty stains spread down the corners of the apartment. The walls were hefty with a century's accumulation of layered wallpaper bubbled into large humps in their centers. The pipe from the stove wobbled up to and through a rip in the ceiling where some industrious derelict had tried to do a patch job by nailing flattened beer cans over the gaps. It was altogether the sort of place that a man with serious money would not even enter, a man with pin money would not linger in, but a man with no money would have to call home. For a while.

"Suze," Jewel called. "Bring me a cup of coffee, will ya?"

"What?" Suze yelled. "I can't hear you, I'm in the john."

After a few more slashing strums Jewel gave up on trying to bully a song from the flattop box. He shoved the guitar under the couch. He wore a stag-cut red shirt, shiny black slacks, and sharp-toed cowboy boots. His bare left bicep exposed the wet-ink blur of a cross with starlike points jail-tattooed into his pale skin. His long blond hair was combed up and greasy, sculpted into a style that had been the fashion at about the time of his birth. Jewel, however, had divined an image of himself in his nocturnal wonderings and the atavistic comb work was the key flourish in it.

He called to Suze again. "Well, get out of the john! And bring me a cup of coffee, hear?"

"A cup?"

"Yeah! A cup of coffee, damn it."

Maybe he should have left her back home, Jewel speculated. Let her dodge grease splatters at the Pork Tender Stand for the rest of her life. Give joy to pig farmers at drive-ins on Saturday night and wonder why she'd ever let Jewel Cobb slip away. That would be fitting. He was bringing her along in the world, taking her to Saint Bruno, a city where things can change, but was she grateful?

Not by a long sight. She'd rather paint each of her toenails a different color, or count the pigeons under the bridge, than learn how to cook him a decent meal. Lots of women knew things that she didn't and he might not put up with just a whole lot more of her laziness before he picked up his walking cane and strolled out to pluck some daisies.

Ah, but he couldn't leave her now. He'd come to Saint Bruno to change his life, dip a great big spoon into the fabled gravy train of the city, and if cousin Duncan hadn't been greening him, then tonight could be the first little taste of how sweet that new life could be.

Jewel stood up and looked out the window onto Voltaire Street, a street of front-room appliance repair businesses, discount clothing shops, a pool hall called the Chalk & Stroke, a bail bondsman's office, and two hair salons that promised summer cuts and granite perms.

"I let it cool for you, Jewel." Suze's voice entered the room before her loose-jointed shuffle that advertised her dissatisfaction with mundane physical processes. This body was meant for finer things, she seemed to mime, and fine things could happen with a body like that. She was still prey for pimples, and several smears of pink makeup marked the scenes of the latest attacks. Her hair was black and fell in a tangle past her shoulders, front and back, the longer strands flirting with the deep neckline of her floral-print, showtime summer dress.

She sat the cup on the arm of the couch. "Most like it hot. You must've bit a nerve in your mouth when you was drunk or something. It's just the other way about with you."

"I like to drink it, darlin' girl, not sip it. Not slurp around at it like my teeth was loose and I can't wander too far from the front porch rocker no more."

"Some folks put ice in it. Like a Coke."

"No kiddin'," Jewel said. "I think I've heard of that. Must've saw it on Walter Cronkite."

Suze's shoulders slumped beyond their normal depth. "You shouldn't make fun of me," she said. "Everybody makes fun of me."

"Hmm," Jewel grunted, raising the cup of coffee and draining it in one long pull. But then he remembered Duncan.

"You got the time?" he asked.

3

Suze smirked at him, her hands on her hips in the pose of a barn-dance coquette. "You got the nerve, hillbilly?"

"You got to ask that?" Jewel said with a smile. He patted his hair, still smiling. "Nobody's got to ask that. But could be I ain't got the time."

"It's about quarter past eight."

Jewel glanced out to the street where the buildings blocked what was left of the sun, giving an extra dose of gloom to the scene.

"That about makes it time," he said as he walked to the dresser that buttressed the far wall. He opened the top drawer and raised a short, evil-looking knife with a bumble-bee-striped handle and stuck it, sheath and all, into his rear pocket. "You know my business?"

"It's got to do with Duncan, I would guess."

"Well, you can't know that. Forget you do. It's not something you can know."

He started dealing through the few rags in the drawer until he came to a red towel that was wadded in a ball. When the towel was unwadded he lifted a .32 Beretta from it and holstered it inside his waistband. He pulled the tails of his shirt out and let them dangle.

"Oh, fudge," Suze said. "I see it's still going to be *that* kind of business."

Jewel shrugged, then started toward the door.

"It's still *that* kind of life, darlin' girl."

Jewel was to wait for Duncan on the corner of Napoleon and Voltaire, so he stepped into the Chalk & Stroke and bought a couple of bags of Kitty Clover potato chips and a six-pack of tall-boys. He would, given the choice, rather eat potato chips

4

than steak, and since there was rarely such a choice to ponder, he pretty well lived on Kitty Clover.

He stood inside a phone booth and opened a beer, then began to eat the chips. The street was now awake, busy with people going toward taverns and others staggering home, all of whom avoided the younger denizens, bare-chested in satin jackets, who kicked down the streets waiting for something funny to happen at which they could snort and guffaw, or for something mean to pop up so they could prove meaner and stomp it down. If boredom gave way only to more boredom then, perhaps, they would take it upon themselves to borrow something shiny and custom upholstered in which to escape that chronic state.

No one paid any attention to Jewel Cobb.

Duncan was just on time. He pulled up in a long blue Mercury that was past its prime but still flashy enough for a Willow Creek boy to take horn-honking pride in.

Jewel slid in on the passenger's side.

"Hey, cousin Dunc," Jewel said with a nod. "Nice wheels."

Duncan regarded his younger cousin with some disdain. The boy was country tough, but hillbilly tacky. That shirt was an open admission to cops, citizens, and marks — watch out, I'm trouble.

"You settled right in the middle of it," Duncan said as he pulled into traffic, heading north on the cobblestone street. "Frogtown."

"The price is right."

Duncan was in his late twenties with a neatly molded pot belly and thick, strong arms. There was a placid quality about his pale, sagging features that the ambitious glint of his green eyes served to counterpoint. His clothes were simple: open-necked blue knit shirt, a cream sports jacket, and gray slacks.

5

His wheat-straw hair was cut short but not freakishly so. By careful design there was very little that would cause him to be remembered in a crowd of three or more.

"It's called Frogtown," Duncan said, "because it was French folks who settled it. Run into lots of Frogs hereabouts."

Jewel had gorged on the chips and swallowed most of the beer. He finished it, stuffed the empty under the seat, and opened another.

"Frogs, huh? Why do they call 'em Frogs?"

"I can't say I know. They seem to like water, swamps, and such like. I don't know. It's a saying, like coon, you see? Maybe like redneck." He caught Jewel's eye. "You don't call 'em Frogs to their face, though. If you ain't one, too. You see, it's not as bad as nigger, but it's not good."

"Huh," Jewel said. "I'm always learnin'."

As they traveled, they left the close-in, crowded jumble of buildings and entered an area that was more spacious but no less grim. The river was in sight, a huge presence to the east, and trailers and wooden houses on stilts were flopped as near to the water as possible. They had come only four blocks but it could have been miles.

"This looks like Willow Creek, only with water instead of rocks," Jewel said.

"Only it ain't. And the people in them places ain't Willow Creek kind of folks."

They passed under a railroad bridge as the light faded into dark. Once beyond the bridge Duncan began to count the slim dirt lanes. At the third he turned toward the water. On either side of the lane was a tangled, belching, smelly swamp. Soon a yellow light was seen, then another light that bounced on the water from a dock.

"That's it," Duncan said. He turned off the car and headlights, then faced Jewel. "Now leave the beer here. Pete Ledoux, he's a grown man and won't go for that joyriding style of yours. If I had to bet, that's what I'd bet, anyway."

"Fuck 'im, then."

"I'd rather camp under the outhouse than fuck with Pete Ledoux, boy. You keep that attitude, Jewel. You keep it." Duncan sighed, a troubled man. "If you wasn't kin I'd deal you out right now."

"I need the dough, that's all."

"Then act like you deserve the chance to get it. Opportunity's knockin' on your thick skull, boy. This ain't the annual Willow Creek–Mountain Grove dustup, Jewel. We're fixin' to tree a fella and tack his hide on the side of the barn. There's folks that won't like that, don't you know? You can't be lousin' it up."

"Yeah," Jewel said. His jaw jutted defiantly, as if this were a commonplace enterprise for him. "Don't be tellin' me what's wrong with me, Dunc. You know and I know why I'm in on this."

"Run that by me again."

" 'Cause I shoot to hurt and I come to shoot, that's why."

Duncan stared at Jewel, then smiled proudly.

"You ain't smart, Jewel, but I can't say as you're dumb, neither." He opened the car door. "Let's go."

Ledoux's house was a sturdy, winterized weekender's cottage bordered by screened-in porches. From the rear door a planked walkway curved down to the dock about fifty feet away.

Duncan knocked on the door.

A woman with a pretty face that had begun to bloat and tousled blond hair swung the door open, revealing a porch overrun by fishing poles, milk cartons, and sporting magazines. She had the expression of one who is intent on being constantly disappointed, and held a can of beer in her hand. She looked at Duncan, then Jewel.

"My word," she said. "We don't often get encyclopedia salesmen out here."

"I expect not," Duncan said. "I've come to see Pete."

"I wouldn't've bought none anyway, just cut out a few of the pictures." The woman gestured with her head, snapping it toward the light that shone on the water. "Saint Francis of the Marais du Croche is down there rappin' with the fishes."

Duncan smiled at her. She was a drinker with good looks picking up speed downhill, which was his usual game, but she was Pete's woman.

"Thanks."

"You fellas want a beer, or anything?"

"No thanks."

"That's good, 'cause we ain't got enough to share, anyhow," she said as she closed the door.

The walkway swayed underfoot as they crossed it to the dock. The needle of light was playing on the water, illuminating a great bog of murk and brackish water.

"Say, Pete," Duncan called. "I got my cousin, Jewel, here to meet you."

"Hiya," Pete said, then stuck the beam of light in Jewel's face.

Jewel tried to screen his eyes, then turned his face away.

"Say, hey, man! You learn that trick in the cops, or what?" Pete aimed the light between himself and Duncan.

"Nasty lookin' pup, ain't he?" Pete said.

These fellas aren't handing me much respect, Jewel thought. He'd whipped two men at a time who were bigger than them before. That time in Memphis there'd been three bargemen on a spree and he'd come out of that one pretty good, too, once his tongue had been stitched back together.

"I ain't a pup," Jewel said. He raised his shirttails and exposed the handle of the pistol. "See that there? That's what says I ain't. It can say it six times, too."

Ledoux exchanged glum glances with Duncan. He then walked to a pillar of the dock and flipped an unseen switch. Lights lit up the dock and the men. Ledoux motioned for the others to follow him as he ambled to the edge of the dock.

"I got some catfish to tend to," Ledoux said. He was a short man, well into middle age but still supple and quick. His skin was tanned to match mud, and his brown hair had fingers of gray running through it. He bent to one knee and reached over the edge of the dock to the water. When he stood he pulled a stringer of channel cat and bullhead up. The fish made a weighty, wet splat when he tossed them onto a wooden bench beneath the brightest light.

Without looking away from the fish, he asked Jewel, "You know what you're supposed to do?"

"Sort of. I'm gonna cool out some kind of a porn king."

Ledoux slowly swiveled to face Duncan. When their eyes met he nodded once, then grinned snidely, as if some little-believed prediction of his had come true.

Duncan lowered his eyes, inspecting the toe of his shoe. "He ain't king of his own cock, Jewel. He just owns a theater."

Ledoux spat on the dock near Duncan's feet. "What you're supposed to do, which you 'sort of' know, is kill a nigger and get away with it. 'Sort of' gettin' away with it used to be good enough, back in '37 or so, but the Kennedys and ol' Johnson done shit in that bowl of soup. So, you see, mon ami, 'sort of' wasn't the way I'd planned it to be."

"I went over it with him," Duncan said. "He's game. More than game, ain't you, Jewel?"

"I'm a Cobb, ain't I?" Jewel replied with tremulous bravado.

Ledoux had taken the fish off the stringer and now, one by one, he began to drive nails through their heads, tacking them to the bench. There were a few odd grunts from the fish, which Ledoux seemed to echo. He then raised a knife and inserted the tip beneath the tail fin of each, and, with short, gentle strokes, gutted them. The guts drooped over the side of the bench and hung toward the deck.

Ledoux looked up from his work. "I like fish," he said.

Jewel's head bobbed. "No shit," he said.

Duncan gave Jewel a rough shove. "Tell him what you're going to do, boy! You can come up tough on your own time, but now you're making *me* look bad, hear?"

After straightening himself, as if considering revolt, Jewel relaxed slightly.

"Right," he said. Reality seemed to hug his thoughts and he smiled at the comfort of the embrace. "Sure. This is business. I'm *all* business."

Ledoux was bent over the fish, sticking his hands into their body cavities and ripping out the clinging organs.

"Now you're talkin', mon ami," he said as he flipped a handful that splashed in the darkness beyond the arc of light.

"Duncan told me everything. About twenty-seven times, at least. I got it down, man."

"It really ain't all that involved," Duncan said. "Point it and go boom. He ought to have it down."

"That's very comforting," Ledoux said. "That is very comforting. I'll have that to cherish, for about a quarter-to-life over in Jeff City, there. 'Point it and go boom.' It's good to know we got us such a simple murder, 'cause I can name eight or ten other fellas I know who must've drew tougher jobs. Mon Dieu, if they only saw it as clear as you do, they wouldn't be pressin' boxer shorts for the state."

"Geez, Pete," Duncan said, his voice flat, with only his lips moving. "You don't have to make a speech out of it. You got concerns, then you mention 'em."

"Why, thank you," Ledoux replied, as if honored by some rare privilege. "I do believe I have a concern or two, there, Judge Cobb." He pointed a finger at Jewel. "For instance, does he know this deal cold?"

"No," Jewel said, and swaggered forward. "Look at my ears, buddy. They're too small to be on a dog, see? That means I can talk for myself. And now you bring it up, there is one important thing I don't know cold." He jabbed a finger at Ledoux's chest. "What'm I gettin' exactly? Duncan here, cousin Dunc, he's been a little confusin' with the numbers."

"Well," Ledoux said, "this is beginnin' to make some sense. You're just getting started with us. Fifteen hundred bucks is what you get. That's about ten times what I got when I decided to grow up. It'll all be hidden on the Micheaux Construction payroll."

"I won't do any of that kind of work, though," Jewel said. "I didn't bus up here to strain and sweat for no paycheck."

"This *kid*," Ledoux said, tapping a finger to his temple, "he's really ready for a step up from stealin' eggs from chickens?"

Duncan shrugged, impassive and bored. Ledoux turned back to Jewel.

"You. You're a tough kid, right, mon ami? I'm just curious about the generation gap, you know, that sort of thing. I was wonderin' — what've you ever *done*?"

"Nothin' that ain't strictly my own business, that's what. Mainly."

After nodding, Ledoux returned to the task of cleaning the fish.

Duncan walked over and stood next to Jewel, then began to jab him in the short ribs with his finger. Jewel walked away.

"Okay," Ledoux said. "I've got instincts that it don't pay to fight. You could be right for us, Cobb. Everybody deserves a chance, you know." Ledoux sat on a bloodless section of the bench. "Now the reason you get a payroll check is so we can all run fakes on the taxman, see? He's worse than any cop you ever saw. Any *six* cops you ever saw. I ever get got, it's goin' to be some Kraut with an addin' machine, not some Mick with a badge who does it to me."

Slowly, Jewel nodded. He'd seen that on TV. IRS. Capone, seems like they did it to him. And most of the other big boys went up when their math became criminally inaccurate.

"That's smart," Jewel said, finally. The sophistication of such financial transactions increased his attraction to this line of work.

"I want to tell you one thing first," Ledoux said. He picked up a squat flashlight and began to shine it across the water. The outlines of trees, tips of floating logs, undulations of green scum that roiled on the water's surface, and phantom eye reflections were caught in the beam. "That there — you know what it is?"

"I just hit town," Jewel said. "I ain't learned every backwater."

"That's a hell of a backwater, mon ami. It's the Marais du Croche. That means 'Crooked Swamp' in the tongue. It's a big, endless black bugger, too. Full of sinkholes and slitherin' things and sloughs that go in circles, and every part of it looks so much like every other part of it that most folks, they can't

12

remember which is which, or which way is out, or nothin'. So they get confused. Many times they get confused unto death, mon ami, then in the spring they wash down and land at the dam, bone by bone."

"I been in woods before, with big trees and hooty owls and all that shit, man."

"Not like that." Ledoux flashed the light high and low, slowly displaying a great meanness of which he had somehow grown fond. "You know who knows their way around over there, Cobb?"

Jewel looked at Duncan, then at Ledoux's weathered face.

"I'm goin' to guess *you*."

"Très bien." Ledoux shone the light on Jewel once more. "Me and two or three other old Frogtown boys. That's it. You get in there, no one else can help you but them and me, and they don't know you."

Jewel folded his arms across his chest, then rocked back on his heels and squinted into the light.

"I ain't got no plans to go in there."

"I know. And as long as you do right, I won't ever have to *put* you in there, either. Understand what I'm sayin'?"

Jewel nodded solemnly but did not reply.

"So you're goin' to cool that coon, Crane, on Seventh outside of his theater. Tomorrow afternoon, am I right?"

"As rain and mother-love," Jewel replied.

"This is our special secret, right, Jewel?" Duncan said. "That juggy gal of yours ain't clued in, is she?"

"Are you kiddin'? You got to be kiddin'."

Duncan stepped up and heartily slapped Jewel on the back.

"Oh, yeah, now we're in business. What say you run up to the car and break out that beer you been savin', cuz? We'll cement this deal."

"That's a hell of a notion," Jewel said, and started up the wooden walkway to the car.

Duncan and Ledoux watched him. When the overhead light in the Mercury went on, Ledoux nudged Duncan.

"Him bein' your cousin — that a problem for you?"

"No," Duncan replied, shaking his head. "He's an asshole."

Ledoux began to pile the skinned fish in order to carry them to the house.

"Wonderful," he said. "We've got to be on time and I think he might be one peckerwood who's just barely dumb enough to pull the trigger when we want him to."

"When it comes to dumb, bet on him," Duncan said, as he watched Jewel coming back down the walkway. "If you had a Sears catalogue of dummies you couldn't order a better one. I mean, the punk's just perfect for us."

2

Detective Rene Shade, dressed casually in a black T-shirt and jeans, sat on a stool in the corner of the room and contemplated the patrons of Tip's Catfish Bar. He saw red-faced men with untamed cigarettes bucking their hands through the air; squinty-eyed men who huddled in booths and had professional flinches that drew their heads to the side; white-haired men with fists as gnarled as ancient roots and with expressions mutely wise and unafraid. Few women and no squeamish men gathered here.

Shade's brother owned the bar, and this, too, was on his mind. It had sometimes been an embarrassment at Headquarters for Shade, having to admit that, yes, the Tip Shade who ran the Catfish Bar and welcomed felons, petty thieves, and their apprentices was his older brother. He had tried to explain that the bar was the center of the neighborhood in which they had grown up, and the regulars were neighbors

15

first and threats to society second. It was more personal, not at all clear-cut, where the line could, or even should, be drawn. Such explanations were regarded as suspiciously metaphysical by his superiors. It did not help that his father, the regionally notorious John X. Shade, was prominent in what he insisted upon calling sporting circles, and others, with equal insistence, termed the gambling fraternity.

The bar was built of rough wood on a mound overlooking the river. Oak beams pressed the roof above their heads, while fishnets with cork floaters, a mystifyingly fey decorating touch, dripped down between the beams. The chairs and tables were all wooden, and squeaked with use. There were athletic prints on the walls and photos of local champions. A large mural of Tip hung behind the bar. In it he was poised to hurl his two hundred and thirty some pounds into a spider-legged halfback; holding an intercepted ball aloft in the end zone; and snarling down at a shell-shocked fullback whom he'd crumbled on the one yard line. There was a team picture of the Saint Bruno Pirates, the local minor league baseball team, and a small picture of Eldon Berenger, who'd played one season of basketball in the Continental League. There were several boxers represented. Just to the rear of one stout oak pillar there was a small photo of Rene Shade, gloved hands held above his head as he celebrated a victory in the early, hopeful days of his former career. Near the entrance there was a larger picture of Shade, one taken near the end of the night that the Light-Heavy Champ, Foster Broome, had chased him with a posse of left jabs until his face split up and retreated in different directions to elude pursuit. Shade could not avoid looking at this reminder of his almost glorious past, but every time he did so his stomach tightened up. The picture was one of Tip's attempts at rugged good humor, but Shade rarely managed to smile at it.

16

As Shade watched, Tip poured a double shot of bourbon and pulled a draw for a lanky hustler named Pavelich, who'd once bowled the best game in town, but now regularly bowled the second best for better side money. Tip shoved him his change, then walked down to Shade's end of the bar.

"Another rum, li'l blood?" Tip asked in his slow but somehow belligerent voice.

"But of course. Put it on your bill."

Tip smiled and raised a bottle of Jamaican dark and poured a healthy dollop into Shade's glass.

"Free rum is one thing, drivin' my business away would be another. You lookin' for somebody, or just lonesome to mix with your peers?"

"Have I ever busted anybody in here?"

"Thankfully, no. Or I'd have to bust you."

There was more in that comment than sibling rivalry, Shade thought. Tip always had acted as if he could punish Shade whenever there was a need to. Shade conceded that it could be true. At one seventy, he was outweighed by about sixty pounds, had an advantage in speed but none in unrefereed experience, and knew that their battle hearts were of equal girth.

Shade smiled and nodded.

"I haven't busted any of this crowd, but I could easy enough." He turned on his chair to view more of the room. "I could make six busts on my way to the pisser."

"And lose the goodwill of your neighbors and childhood playmates, li'l blood."

"I could probably pop you, Tip, if I spent ten or twelve minutes in the effort."

Tip began to nod, then shook his head. "I could be eight kinds of crooked, there, piglet, but I ain't never been no kind of dumb."

Shade wondered, for perhaps the thousandth time, what his older brother might've become had his knees held out for more than two memorable seasons of college ball.

"Genes will tell," Shade said.

"What's that mean?"

"Ah, I can't be sure, but I'd be a more confident man if I was."

Tip moved down the bar to tend to a group of men who'd begun shaking their empty mugs at him.

Shade returned to his contemplation of the clientele. He'd known many of them since his childhood, had teamed with them in sandlot games of every sort, sparred with them beneath the elms of Frechette Park on cool summer mornings, and clustered with them at Catholic Church dances where they shared whiskey cleverly secreted in Coke bottles. He'd fought them in the crowded-alley scraps of youth that still seemed more important than those of adulthood, run errands for the older men, and watched as their daughters were happily married off to outsiders, returning to Frogtown only for very short holidays and funerals.

A compact hand nudged him on the shoulder, rousing him from a nostalgia he wasn't sure he believed in.

"Rene. Don't see you much these days. What're you up to tonight?"

It was Wendell Piroque, a keg-shaped teamster who had probably steered more blackjacks than trucks. Shade had known him since grade school, when Piroque had hung out at his mother's poolroom.

"Just drinkin' on Tip."

"Lucky for you," Piroque said, resting on the next stool. "A good brother to have, a bartender is." Piroque had a sweet, round face, with dark features, and his smile was all innocence. "And your mother runs a poolroom. Must be the Irish half of you, gives you that luck."

"Must be. There are no famous sayings about Frogs having it."

"Not in this town, anyhow," Piroque said as he tapped a finger on the bar surface. He suddenly pointed toward the pool table at the rear of the room, a table that was mysteriously underused. "Shoot a game?"

"You got the table roll figured or something?"

"Would I do that to you?" Piroque asked in mock horror.

"You'd do it to yourself, I think, if you could be two chumps at once."

Shade led the way through the maze of tables, nodding at those who nodded at him, saying hello twice, and being stared down once.

"Nine ball?" Piroque asked when they reached the table.

"If you insist," Shade said. "But you might as well just hand me your cash."

Piroque was bent over the green felt, his tongue peeking from the side of his mouth, studiously racking the balls.

"I think different," he said.

"That's good," Shade said. He was a broad-shouldered, dark-skinned, chronically fit man, not youthful but still young, and his blue eyes lit up with the prospect of competition. "That's what keeps me interested enough to hang on to the planet."

The two uniformed patrolmen entered the Catfish at a few minutes past 1 A.M. The larger of the two was a black man who loomed over his squat partner. As they approached the bar the squalling conversations dropped to a whisper, then silence. The patrolmen attempted to meet the glares of the patrons to show command of the situation, but found that two pairs of eyes cannot upstage thirty, and that their erect postures and imitative confidence were seen as comic acting rather than cool control.

The bartender stood with his arms folded, his upper lip hidden by his lower in a warning pout.

"Hey, Shade," the squat patrolman said. "Your brother here?"

Tip sneered, then swung his head upward, indicating the back of the room.

"There he is," the black patrolman said. "At the pool table."

Shade leaned on his cue as he watched the blue aliens approach. He scanned the layout on the table, then turned to meet them. Before they could speak, he said, "One more inning and I got it bagged."

The smaller patrolman shook his head. "Captain Bauer says now."

Piroque overapplied English and threw off an attempted combo of the six-nine. He straightened, scraped chalk on the cue tip, and smiled at Shade.

"You could forfeit," he said. "If duty calls."

"No," Shade said. He stepped up to the table, calculated the odds on his running out, then bent over to shoot. With his left arm bulging lean muscles like twisted brown taffy he poised to stroke. "Six ball," he said, and sank it, the high left on the cue ball carrying it to the far rail.

"Captain's waitin'," the short beat man said. "What's it goin' to cost you?"

"Nothing," Shade said. He had a hope, and it involved a bank shot combination, for a run-out was stymied by the far-flung eight ball. "Seven-nine. In the corner, just in case I make it I'll have witnesses." He positioned himself for the shot, stroked the cue ball dead on, with no English, and watched as the seven ball banked across the table and did just what it was meant to do — kick the nine ball gently into the pocket.

He turned to Piroque, whose hand was already in his wallet.

"Save it, Wendell. Get your kid a model airplane."

"Uh-uh," Piroque said, shaking his head. "When you come up short, you got to shell out." He handed Shade a five-dollar bill without ceremony. "You shoot decent stick, Shade. I'll give you that. But I got to tell you, you still ain't good enough to hold your old man's chalk, you know?"

"Thanks, Wendell," Shade said.

"Detective," the talkative patrolman said, his foot leaving the ground in a weak stomp of insistence. "It shouldn't be takin' us this long."

Shade followed the uniforms toward the door, conscious of the near silence, and the truculent presence of Tip's eyes upon him. At the bar Tip beckoned to him by crooking a finger.

"Yeah?" Shade said.

Tip leaned toward him, then did a threatening flex of his massive arms. "Keep your new friends out of here." Tip's blunt-featured, pockmarked face was expressionless, but his brown eyes were flat with anger. "You can play with them in the street, but not in the house, understand?"

"Why don't you bounce them?"

Tip glared at Shade. "You owe me for the rum now, smart-ass," he said, rearing back. "It decided not to be free."

"I got business," Shade said and walked toward the door.

Tip came around the bar like it was a pudgy high school lineman and Shade a passing quarterback. The two patrolmen dropped their fingers onto the handles of their street-issue pacifiers. They looked around nervously as the brothers confronted each other.

"Stay the fuck out of here if you're goin' to cause me trouble," Tip said. He clenched his fist and waved it vaguely in Shade's direction. "I told you, you cost me business and I'll drop-kick your ass, brother or not."

After scraping his fingers beneath his chin, an ancient taunt, Shade said, "When you feel froggy, start jumping, bro."

Tip opened his mouth to retort, then looked at the uniforms and took a backward step. He nodded several times.

"Been a pleasure seein' you, Rene. Drop me a postcard along about Armageddon, hear?"

Shade turned away, then paused before the large, prominent picture of himself in a bruised and humbled state.

"Next time I come callin', Tip, it'd be good if that was gone."

"Naw. It's my favorite," Tip said in a strained whisper. "'Cause it's you to a tee, li'l blood. It's you to a tee."

Shade looked back at the picture and studied it complacently. Finally he shrugged and threw up his hands. "It's everybody once in a while," he said, then walked out the door.

Some of the blood had splattered the television set. Detective How Blanchette craned his neck over the expensive RCA and looked on the table behind it. There were flecks of gray and chunks of white visible in the smears of red.

"Looks like he was turnin' the channel or somethin', is what would be my guess," he said. "If I was paid for guessin' I'd be done."

The patrolman to whom he'd spoken did not respond. He was transfixed by the crumpled body of a middle-aged black man, a man who'd been ruined by the sudden excavation of the back of his head.

"You spot any clues in the body language, there, Cooper?" Blanchette asked. Blanchette was sandy-haired and fat, and he insisted on wearing, at almost all times, a black leather trench coat that he believed slimmed his image by twenty pounds. "Maybe Rankin died in the shape of a letter of the alphabet to tip us off, huh? That look like an 'm' or a 'z' to you?" Cooper looked away. "Could be, though, that he was usin' deaf-talk sign language, huh, Cooper? All the politicians use it now."

Cooper finally met Blanchette's eyes.

"You got a soft heart, How," Cooper said. "Almost squishy." Cooper held his hands up, then began to wander about the room. It was nicely decorated, a den with ornate lamps and polished mahogany furniture. He shook his head. "I knew this man. I was on his stinkin' bodyguard detail, you know, back when that busin' thing got nasty." He paused with his back to the body. "He treated me pretty fuckin' decent. Not like a butler who carries a gun, you know. Fuckin' decent."

Blanchette nodded, apparently in sympathy. "Somebody didn't think him so decent, though, is what I would think. What with my nine years' experience and all, I'd have to say that could be a fact. I'd say you should get out your black notebook, there, the one full of blank pages, and start one of 'em out with — Alvin Rankin, city councilman, was whacked in the head by someone who didn't think he was so fuckin' decent."

"I'll be outside," Cooper said. "You miserable tub of guts."

Blanchette held up a hand to halt him.

"That'll be Detective Sergeant miserable-tub-of-guts to you, there, patrolman."

"Check," Cooper said and went outside.

Blanchette surveyed the room, his dark eyes taking in the scene, his thick brows flexing as he concentrated. The room was a reluctant witness. For a crime scene, which it indisputably was, it set new levels of tidiness. Other than the blood and body fallout necessary to qualify it, Blanchette thought, the place could win a Good Housekeeping Seal for most meticulous murder site. The only thing out of place besides the wrecked remains of Alvin Rankin was the *TV Guide* that had landed about two feet to the right of Rankin's outstretched hand.

As Blanchette speculated on the possibilities offered by the slim clues on the scene, the door from the main room opened and Captain Karl Bauer entered the den, followed closely by a pack of crime specialty men.

Bauer was a large, square man with hair the color of carp scales, still loyally fashioned into a flattop. He had stern features, and knobby fists, but many of his subordinates believed him to be an incompetent police officer. His talent as a political infighter, however, was undeniable, and he was a truly gifted backslapper.

Captain Bauer walked past Blanchette and stood with his back to him.

"The wife and the girl are across the street, at 605. Neighbors named Wilkes. Give them time to have a shot of whiskey or some coffee, then get over there."

"Right," Blanchette said. "She say anything else?"

"I wouldn't keep it a secret if she did, Detective. She came home from seeing *Raiders of the Lost Ark* with the girl—" Bauer flipped through his notepad to find the daughter's name. "Janetha, aged seventeen. It was about eleven forty-five or so." Bauer closed the notepad and put it in his breast pocket. "End of dialogue."

"I think maybe his wallet is gone," Blanchette said. "It ain't layin' around nowhere."

"His wallet? You break in a house, kill a city councilman with a Mercedes and a stash of chink vases, and you just take his wallet? That make sense to you? I mean, the rest of the house hasn't even been walked through, from the looks of it."

"Well," Blanchette said. "Guys who ain't used to splatterin' people's brains, they do funny things when it finally happens, sir. The French have a word for it, but I don't know it, so I call it freakin' out."

"That's one possibility," Bauer said. He turned toward the other officers in the room and held both hands pointed at them, then began to click his fingers. "You guys get busy. Fariello, get plenty of shots," he said to the photographer. Bauer had watched this scene in many movies and directed the rest of the crime squad action in a Rich Little–type whirl of unconscious imitation.

Blanchette shook his head as he watched his captain. He nodded his treble-chinned moon face whenever he noted obvious influences on Bauer's behavior. That's Broderick Crawford, there. Oh, that bark's familiar, there's more than a hint of Bogart in it. That steely glare, seems like Matt Dillon traded on it for a fortune in reruns. Where's Kojak?

Finally Bauer returned to Blanchette.

"Where's Shade?" he asked.

"I'm not on Shade watch this week, Captain."

Bauer stared down at him. "You know, Blanchette, for a short guy you're awful fat—anybody ever tell you that?"

"No person now living, sir. A gentleman wouldn't say it anyway, I know that from reading the 'Dear Abby' in the paper."

"So, you're a literate man, Blanchette. Have another doughnut and you'll be two of them." Bauer started toward the door, then stopped. "I'm going over to the mayor's house. He'll want to be kept informed by the tick-tock on this. When Shade manages to get here you and him talk to the wife and girl, then meet me on Second Street."

"Sure, Captain."

In the front room, between the den and the main door, was a large, overstuffed, underused leather chair. Blanchette sank into it, then lit a cigar and waited for Shade. As he smoked he thought about Alvin Rankin. About forty-four, forty-five, a product of Pan Fry, Saint Bruno's historically black section; smart and tough, blessed with the rare talent to know who to be tough to and who to outsmart; a coming power of the Democratic Party, with increasing clout as Pan Fry residents began to actually vote, rather than put X's where told to and stay quiet the rest of the decade. Alvin Rankin could have been, Blanchette knew, the first black mayor of Saint Bruno. That was motive number one in flashing neon. The banner of social advancement did not wave at the head of a unanimous throng, and Saint Bruno was, and had long been, a city of tenacious suspicions and disparate convictions. Saint Brunians were imbued with an unfriendly blend of ancestral pride, selfish toughness, and purposeful ignorance that served to produce succeeding generations of only slightly less narrow views than the generation that had laid the bricks that still paved the streets.

Blanchette stared toward the room in which Rankin's future had been diverted. Yes, he could've made it, all right, Blanchette thought. Not with his next breath or two, but by the time he was fifty, fifty-five. It was up to someone else now.

The end of his cigar had a thumb of ash on it, so Blanchette flicked it on the rug, then rubbed it in with his foot. He looked around the room, feeling slightly outclassed by the numerous objets d'art and fashion that he could not even name. Yup, pretty swell place for a smoke who'd never moved away to sing in falsetto or shoot balls through hoops. Hard hustle to get here in this hometown.

Shade walked in and Blanchette stood up.

"Glad you could make it, Shade. Didn't interrupt you in

something important, I hope. You know, like a date with that slinky brunette you been seein', there — the one who moves like her back ain't got no bone. What's her address again?"

Shade moved past Blanchette without an answer and entered the den. At the sight of Rankin's body there was a tremor of weakness through his legs. It was unprofessional, he knew, but the shockingly limp postures of the dead were something he would never be hardened to. To make this one more meaningful was the fact that he'd known Rankin slightly.

"Didn't take any chances, did they?" he said.

"No," Blanchette said. He moved with a pugnacious waddle that had a limber grace to it, despite his build. "Two bullets — zip, zip — in the back of the head. That usually turns the trick."

"Who found him?"

"His wife and daughter. They're across the street."

"Bauer been here?"

"Just left. He went to hold the mayor's hand till the bogeyman leaves his dreams."

Shade examined the room, stepping around the photographer and the fingerprint boys.

"Damn clean piece of work," Shade said. His brown hair was long, combed back on top, and he brushed at it with his hand, a habit he had when distracted. "It must've been a friend, huh."

"That's a sickeningly liberal definition, there, Comrade Shade, for a guy pumps two bullets in the back of your head."

"It's point-blank," Shade said. "In his den, watching TV. That sounds like they knew each other to me. Knew each other well enough that old Alvin could relax with him. Or her."

Blanchette picked up the *TV Guide* and scrutinized it.

"I'd say he was changin' channels," he said. "He's only been dead an hour, maybe two. That'd be my guess, and from what the wife says it's pretty close."

Shade was listening with only a fraction of his attention. Alvin Rankin's house, his death, his limp body, all put Shade in mind of the Rankin he'd admired since youth. He was much younger than Rankin, but he clearly remembered the audacious teenaged Rankin who'd boldly made the trip down the ridge from Pan Fry toward the river and Frogtown. He'd come alone, and he'd had a proposition for the Frogtown boys: if we all quit pounding each other for sport we'd have less cops around and more spaciousness, you know, and then we could all take care of business. The Sadat of Pan Fry had had a vision and the nerve to give it a try. Shade had been impressed. Of course the older Frogtown boys had stomped the uppity smoke into a near sludge and dumped him from a Chevy at the foot of the Pan Fry hill, but ever since then Shade had paid attention to Rankin's career. He had been a man to watch, always.

Blanchette tapped Shade on the shoulder.

"Looks to me like he was turnin' from 'Nightline,' there. Must've got bored hearin' how the Israelis and PLO still won't kiss and make up, even though we're all anxious for the wedding party. So he gets up to turn to something else." Blanchette flicked a thumbnail on the guide. "I'd say he was switchin' over to forty-one for the late movie, which was *The Good Humor Man*."

"Why do you figure that? Or is it just a chubby guy's intuition?"

Blanchette held his hands to the sky and shrugged.

"That's what I'd've turned to. I loved that movie when I was a kid. 'Niat pac levram.' Saw it at the old Fox, you know."

"I'd forgotten that, How," Shade said. "That was 1953,

28

wasn't it? I remember I went to the library that day, instead."

"Yeah," Blanchette said. "You got that book, *101 Bad Jokes,* didn't you? Then you memorized it."

Shade began moving the furniture, searching for shell casings. He was getting the details of the room straight in his mind.

"There's no sign of forced entry?" he asked.

"None. Not unless a delinquent genie misted through the keyhole. No scratches on the locks, no crowbar work."

The intimacy of such crimes, the friend with a gun, a grudge, and the natural opportunities to get even, gave them an aspect of tragedy that other crimes lacked.

"It had to be someone he knew and trusted."

"Rene," Blanchette said, "he was black, but he was still a pol, you know. They play the game just like Irish ward bosses, or German congressmen, buddy. It's their job to be approachable by people with a vote. That's why they get the vote. All that does, far as I can see, is narrow it down to members of his own party."

"That," Shade said, "is a suggestion that will no doubt have the county chairman giggling shrilly into his brandy snifter."

With her hands spread on either side of herself, Mrs. Cleo Rankin leaned back on the couch, her head held high, and met Shade's gaze with unmistakable suspicion. Her hair was feathered at the sides and back, with a wave on top. Mocha skin was contrasted skillfully with red glossy lipstick and white jewelry.

"That's everything I told the captain. That's all there is."

"Did Janetha notice anything?" Shade asked.

"She came in behind me. I'm not certain that she even clearly saw — what I saw. She's upstairs now."

"Alvin carry a lot of cash on him?" Blanchette asked

abruptly. "Was it a habit of his to flash a roll down at the corner store, places like that?"

Cleo's eyes darkened.

"After he'd parked his pink Cadillac, you mean?" she asked.

"I didn't mean that," Blanchette said with no apology in his tone. "But his wallet is gone. It's the only thing that is, too."

Cleo slid her glance from the detectives and studied the wall.

"I don't think he was killed for his wallet," she said.

"But we all know that even two hundred or so is pretty attractive around here," Shade said.

"You mean that's the price of murder here, amongst us degenerates of Pan Fry? That *is* what you mean?"

"Or Frogtown," Shade said. "Or a lot of other places with prettier names."

Cleo lifted her head and paused, then made a decision. She reached into her black leather handbag on the couch beside her. Her hand came out clutching a beige wallet.

"It was in his pocket," she said, and handed it to Shade.

"Mrs. Rankin," Shade said. "Did you tamper with anything else over there? It's important to know." Crimes were tough enough, Shade thought, without misdirections created by family members of the victim. "It would've been better if you'd left it there."

Blanchette stood next to Shade as they examined the wallet.

"Empty," Blanchette said. "The friend who nailed him was a triple threat — friend, killer, and thief."

"No," Cleo said. "Here." She pulled a wad of cash from her purse and extended it to Shade. "I took the money out of the wallet."

"Why did you do that?"

Cleo's face became taut, then bitter. "I didn't want the first police on the spot to have a big scuffle over who gets it, that's why!"

"Hunh," Shade grunted. He knew there were thieves in uniform, cops who picked up a few watches at suicide scenes, and a bottle or two of liquor that seemed to be handy. He'd seen it happen once, and that cop wouldn't be doing it again. "That was the first thing that occurred to you when you saw your man smeared on the floor?"

Cleo flinched. She picked a cigarette from the pack on the coffee table, and lit it with a heavy silver lighter. "Alvin was successful and I've always been thankful for that. You don't know how thankful. But because of his work we never left Pan Fry. And I've never forgotten that I grew up here, know what I mean?"

"Yes," Shade said. "I think maybe I do."

"When I was a girl we lived over here about four blocks, with a patch of mud for a yard and three families in the house. One day I was helping my grandmother make a mulberry cobbler. Her heart gave up while she was carrying the cobbler to the oven. She dropped, the cobbler dropped, and I went screaming for help. I was fifteen," she said with a rueful laugh. "Old enough to know better. But I didn't. Finally two police-men came. I still remember one of them named Burris. Ugly redhead, you know, with freckles like a disease. Well, they stood over grandmother and looked down at her awhile, then said, 'Auntie Sally, she ain't gonna finish that cobbler.' They started looking around the room. It was amazing that I was the only one home that day, and they walked around the house until they came to a big old carved clock we had. It'd been in the family for years. 'Go down to Lehman's Store and call the dinge ambulance,' Burris said. And I did, like that might help her somehow. When I got back the police were gone, grandmother was still laying where I'd left her, and there was a big empty spot where the clock used to be."

There was silence, then Blanchette shuffled his feet and raised himself from against the wall where he'd slouched.

"What a sad story," he said. "Where're the Kleenex?"

"See?" Cleo said, pointing at Blanchette. "I probably saved the peace by hiding that cash. He'd pocket it in a minute."

After hooking his thumbs in his belt loops, Blanchette rocked back on his heels and grimaced.

"It'd be my job to collect evidence," he said. "I think it's page 201, or in there. That's the manual, and I live by the book. Anybody can see that."

Cleo stood and smoothed her skirt. She walked to the door and held it open.

Shade stuffed the cash into the wallet, then followed her to the door.

"I really have nothing more to say," Cleo told them.

"Sorry for your tragedy, there," Blanchette said as he passed her and stepped out onto the lawn.

Blue and red lights twirled in the night, and white uniforms were moving a sheet-covered litter from out of the house across the street. Many voices filled the air, some terse, some entertained, and some angry. A crowd had gathered, but it was largely silent, listening to the officials on the scene.

"Get some rest," Shade said.

"You just do your job."

"You don't even have to tell us that, lady," Blanchette snapped.

"Hey," Cleo said. She held her hand out, palm up. "The cash, please."

Shade stroked his hair, and shook his head very slowly.

"You're not going to believe this," he said. "But it's evidence now."

Cleo stiffened and withdrew her hand.

"You are *so* right," she said.

The two detectives studied one another for a moment, then Blanchette shrugged. Shade turned around and handed the wallet to Cleo.

"I don't have to do this," he said. "But I am."

Cleo accepted the wallet, then backed inside the doorway.

"You got some guilt," she said. "That's all it is."

Then she firmly swung the door closed.

3

Shade and Blanchette drove through the streets of Pan Fry, past small wooden homes that wobbled from the century or more of hard living that they'd seen, past three-story group housing where half the apartments had windows rotting out and the other half had neatly painted window boxes full of red and yellow flowers. Occasionally there was a minor leap up-scale, and there would be a prim, crisply clean, color-coordinated house, with a carport and a chain-link fence.

"How," Shade said. "I've got to ask you this. Just what is the edge in rudeness? What advantage do you think it gives you?"

After an amused and amiable grunt, Blanchette said, "I could give a good reason. I know one. I mean, I could say it's because that stirs people up, makes them blurt things that make my job easier. I could tell you that one."

"But you won't."

"Not to you, here in the dark and all alone. I mean, the

truth is, people bug the shit out of me half the time. Their bullshit bores me. I don't mind a little bullshit but, you know, you ought to astonish me with it, not nod me off." Blanchette looked at Shade and winked. "You know that. The ones that really get me are the ones who say, 'Society made me do it,'" Blanchette mimicked. "'I didn't have a bicycle when I was eight, Your Honor, so naturally I can't be blamed for hammerin' nails through the nun's head and rapin' the priest when I was twenty.' Shit, man, I grew up on dirt, and now I work for more of it."

"So nobody else can complain?"

"They can complain all they want, but I don't care."

"You have no sympathy for yourself," Shade said.

"I guess I'd need more college to see the smartness in that silliness, partner."

The street lights became brighter when they'd passed out of Pan Fry. Saint Bruno, with a population of two hundred thousand, was a city of many neighborhoods, Frogtown and Pan Fry being the largest and most fabled, and great numbing stretches of anonymous, bland, and nearly affluent subdivisions.

At Clay Street Blanchette turned east with rubber-squealing confidence and stomped the gas pedal since traffic was light. Pio's Italian Garden was still open, the red neon pizza in the window flashing an all-night invitation. Blanchette found his memories of repasts taken there to be varied but sufficient, and he suddenly wheeled into the parking lot.

He looked at Shade and said, "A man's got to eat. Hungry?"

"For chrissake no, man."

Blanchette climbed from the car, then leaned in the door.

"Tragedy saps your energy, Rene. Does mine anyhow. Think I'll grab a meatball grinder."

"You're a real man, How."

35

Blanchette nodded in agreement, then closed the door and went into Pio's.

For reasons that Shade found to be too tangled to articulate and too elusive to grasp, he liked How Blanchette. That put him in a very small club. But he'd known Blanchette too long, their Frogtown pasts were too interwoven for him not to forgive him, even for the unforgivable.

How had started life in Frogtown, about three alleys north of the Shades, as Arthur Blanchette. His father, the eccentric and locally cherished Leigh Blanchette, had provided material for exuberant, arm-spreading barroom tales, and closely huddled, snide, post-mass anecdotes that were recounted by several generations of Frogtowners, while sticking his son with a nickname that would become both his burden and his distinction.

When How was fifteen and still known as Arthur, the Dunne family, who lived behind them, had given their sons bows and arrows as birthday presents. Soon they had an informal archery range, sending arrows flying toward the bank of dirt that formed the boundary between the Dunne and Blanchette backyards. Pappy Dunne was an Irishman with fantasies of personal talent, enormous tabs at neighborhood taverns, and a job at Jerry's Seat Covers. He wanted his children to be better than he was, better at all things, so one evening after seriously exercising his elbow with several mugs of brew, he decided to show them the proper form of archery. He pulled an arrow back, and aimed it with bold innovation by timing his staggers, then letting it fly at the zenith of his lurch. The fateful arrow cleared the dirt mound by several feet, glided past the trees in the adjacent yard, and crashed through the window of the Blanchettes' TV room.

History would never get it straight, for it was an incident clouded with possibilities from the beginning. But Leigh

Blanchette did come slowly, almost furtively, into the back-yard with the catalyst arrow in his hand. He gave it back to the concerned Pappy Dunne, then reclined on the dirt. It had given him quite a start, he explained, that arrow tearing through the window toward his heart. Handball is all that saved him, he reported. It gave him the reflexes to twist just that necessary bit to the side and allow the razor-tipped vessel of death to pass. Pappy Dunne was drunk but comfortable in that state and mentioned that it was just a blunt-ended kid's arrow that might KO a bird if it caught it just right, but was no real threat to your average accidental target. "Gunsmoke," Pere Blanchette responded. Could it be more than coincidence that he was watching "Gunsmoke" at the exact time when an arrow, a danger that had never before occurred to him, came at him from ambush? That's not on on Tuesdays, Pappy Dunne said. No one was listening.

Within a week Pere Blanchette would explain that he had been mystically chosen by the wily spirits of warriors past and rained upon by arrows of such number and deadly force that all he could do was cross himself in wonder that he had survived. And the really inspirational thing was, he said, that he'd been watching television and it was just at the point where Tom Jeffords and Cochise shake hands in *Broken Arrow* when atavistic combat interceded in his life. Many bottles of red wine were garnered through the elaboration of his tale, and within a month Pere Blanchette had begun to haunt secondhand shops and the Goodwill, searching for Navajo rugs and plaster Indians.

As Shade could well recall, for he and his brothers, Tip and Francois, had been as guilty as any, Arthur Blanchette began to be greeted on the street by upraised palms and grunts of "How." He was portly even then, and his face would redden while his hands clenched. It was well known that if Arthur got you down and dropped the bomb of his weight upon you it would mean victory for him, but it was equally well known that any but the most feeble of leg could outdistance him, and the more talented local hand-on-meat percussionists could do snappy Buddy Rich drumrolls about his head and shoulders before his seeking fist could hit anything solid. So he could not stop the advent of the new name.

Soon he was known only as How, his real name filed away with his lackluster childhood. Eventually he grew to accept his sobriquet after he found out that most great athletes became famous by a name other than the one they were born under. Even presidents were like that, and now so was he.

Shade sat in the dark car, watching headlights glare by on Clay Street, chuckling as he remembered minor histories.

Blanchette returned with a grinder in white wax paper, the red sauce dripping down his overaggressive fingers. He slid behind the steering wheel, then had to retrieve a meatball that he'd popped loose. He found it under the seat and slipped it back into the bun.

"If you didn't wring it like it was a chicken's neck it wouldn't goo all over you, How."

Blanchette bit into the grinder, a large, passionate bite, and chewed it with his mouth writhing in pleasureful smacks.

"Then I might drop it," he said.

"You dropped it anyway."

"Hey, man—I paid for it."

Shade grunted. "That's the crucial fact," he said.

After taking another bite that was a meal in itself, Blanchette nodded.

"I always thought so," he said.

At the corner near the station Shade hopped out of the car and walked while Blanchette pulled around to the parking lot.

There were several cars parked illegally in front of the station and a gaggle of murmuring forms were flocked around the main entrance. Shade bounced his fist off the hood of a gray sedan and gestured to the man inside.

"Park it somewhere else," Shade said.

The man inside yawned at Shade, then flipped his press badge at him.

"I'm from the *Daily Banner,*" he said, as if the words were armor.

Shade objected to his tone.

"They pay your tickets for you? Or are you too rich to care?"

"I'm here on a story, officer. You're a detective, right?"

Shade walked to the driver's window and leaned down. He thumped his fist against the car door and wondered why he had chosen this car to enforce the rules on.

"Mister," Shade said. "I'd hate to have to ticket a conduit to the people, but you might make me do it. See, I don't like being a prick, there, friend." A jab of a smile crossed Shade's face. "But it's my job."

The reporter nodded with resignation.

"We could go on with this dialogue for quite a while, couldn't we?"

"And then I'd ticket you."

"I get it," said the reporter, then turned the key in the ignition.

Shade started up the steps to the station.

There was a collection of newsmen, gore seekers, and minor officials gathered on the steps. A coolly appraising ballgame crowd, their hands jerked to swat the bugs that rendezvoused below the archaic globes of light mounted on either side of the entrance, redundant with hand-painted POLICE. The word of the murder was spreading fast and more people were arriving to loiter on the smooth stone steps that led up to the white rock building.

At the door a hangdog college boy reporter named Voigt, with a cowlick and too many Izod shirts, began to close in on Shade.

"Rene," Voigt said, sidling up with a hand-slapping attempt at familiarity. Then, "Detective Shade, I mean. Any comment on the Rankin murder?"

Shade slowed down, rubbing his hair, and shook his head.

"Who's the other guy from the *Banner*?" he asked, then nodded toward the street.

"What other guy?"

"The guy I just made move his car. Salt-and-pepper hair, skin like wilted lettuce."

Voigt grimaced with understanding.

"Braverman! Damn!" Voigt threw his notepad to the ground. As Shade walked on he heard Voigt say, "I'm fine for covering kids who spray-paint bridges, or old ladies who smack muggers with umbrellas, but when a *good* story comes along . . ."

In the entrails of the building, on a floor waxed to approximate ice, near a door marked MEN that was propped open by a wastebasket that dribbled tan wads of paper, Shade found himself feeling strangely dumb. He was beginning to absorb the implications of the murder of Alvin Rankin. There would be gentle prods from the mount on this case. Spurs to the butt, heat and leverage, necessary doors overtly slammed.

When he passed the duty desk Shade mumbled an unfocused glob of words to the man who occupied it. He was entering the battered green door of the squad room when his name was called.

"What?" he asked the duty officer.

"Blanchette with you?"

"My man is parking the car," Shade said, then started through the swinging green door.

"Hey, Shade. Hold it. The two of you are supposed to go directly to Mayor Crawford's place. Captain said to send you right over — no coffee, no squats in the library. Straight over."

"Did he tell you to call me Shade, too?"

"What? What's with you?"

Something in the man's tone had sounded like a hidden insult, but now Shade felt petty.

"Nothin'," he said. He looked down the long, glazed hall and smiled sardonically. "It's just that some aspects of my adult life disappoint the 'eternal boy' in me."

"Hunh," said the duty officer. "And here I was just thinkin' you were an asshole."

"Now that," Shade said as he stepped down the hall, "is another of the 'eternal boy's' major concerns, if you can believe it."

The officer sat down and swung his feet to the desktop.

"I probably could," he said, "but I think I'll pass."

Blanchette leaned on Shade's arm, a pantomime of crumbling health, and swatted at his thighs in a hit-and-run massage.

"Just left it," he wheezed. "Parked it by the pole, there, you know. The pole in the corner of the lot. I think it's the quarter-mile mark or something. Couldn't Bonehead have radioed?"

Shade pulled from beneath Blanchette's weight.

"They could've."

"We need a union, you ask me. The man thinks he can dispense with technology out of callous disregard for our health. Unions make 'em pay extra, they want to do that."

This time Shade insisted on driving. The streets had evolved

41

through the nighttime cycle, from passageways to minor entertainments and basic sins, rampant with sad revelers and charades of Dubble Bubble bliss, into the emptiness of post-party, the asphalt tickled only by taxis, patrol cars, thieves, and swing-shift nurses. But now the people who gave the bulge to the city's withering bicep had begun to commute with their hands rubbing at the spot behind their eyeballs while splashing a Thermos of scalding joe toward the seat where the cup sat, heading for McDonnell-Douglas, the Salter-Winn Shoe Factory, the dairy, and, again, the hospital. Daylight was only a vague promise in the east, and night had girded itself for a final stand before it welcomed defeat.

Shade picked his way through the drowsy traffic toward Hawthorne Hills, a stretch of mounds that pimpled the southern edge of town, giving refuge to most of the monied and many of the elected of Saint Bruno.

A large white house lounged on a hill like a favorite chair on an afterdeck, one leglike section curled over a ribbon of creek and the other leg crooked around a swath of oaks. Shade pulled into the drive.

Captain Bauer had parked next to the tennis court. Shade parked next to him, and he and Blanchette started toward the door.

He knew that Mayor Crawford had done many things before he entered politics, but having been smart enough to be born rich beyond fear seemed like the experience most relevant to his subsequent career.

Their knock was answered by the mayor. He was in slacks and a polo shirt with a cherry half-robe loosely belted. Fit and silver-haired, he looked like the aging stud of a prime-time soap.

"Come in, officers," he said. He was wearing his job-description grief, his solemnity working overtime. "How is Alvin's family?"

"They're taken care of," Shade said.

"They must be in shock," Crawford murmured with a shake of his head.

"No sir," Blanchette said. "The woman, Rankin, Cleto or whatever, is standin' up solid."

Crawford looked at Blanchette dully.

"Her name is Cleo," he said. "And she must certainly be shocked. You may not be, but I am as well."

"What would shock How," Shade said, "would turn thousands gray."

"I see," Crawford said. "How Blanchette, hunh. Leigh's boy — am I right?"

"Yes, sir. Before I got to be two hundred pounds of short-fused earthquake, I was Leigh's boy."

Crawford laughed, then rubbed his mouth with his hand.

"Must be getting a cold," he said. "I remember Leigh. Used to hear about him down at St. Peter's, about every third mass."

Blanchette grimaced, then put his hands in his pockets.

"I'm sure you did, sir."

"He had, well, sort of an interesting mind, your father."

"I really don't want to hear about it."

Crawford's hackles did not even rise, the self-restraint of the indigenous lord confronted by a sulky serf. He smiled indulgently.

"Of course, Blanchette," he said softly, "I can well imagine that you wouldn't want to share such fond memories of your own dear father."

After wincing, Blanchette looked away, toward the captain.

"I'm thinkin' somebody ought to be monitorin' the radio, there, Captain."

"Sure," Bauer said. He waved from where he sat, surrounded by the regal brocade of a chair that could sleep two in a pinch. "That might be wise."

"I'm sure of it," Blanchette said.

As he went out the door, Crawford said, "My pleasure."

When the door closed Shade said, "He's a good man."

"Damn near two of them is what I say," Bauer cut in. "Haw, haw."

Shade looked about the room, trying to guess how many basketballs he could swap one of the ashtrays for. He wondered why he was there. No one seemed to want to ask him much.

"Shade," Bauer was saying. "This is Detective Rene Shade."

"Another familiar name," Crawford said.

"I don't think we've met."

"I don't recall it either." Crawford poured two cups of coffee from a silver service that occupied a shelf above the piano. He handed a cup to Shade. "Black?"

"That's fine."

"I have to sleep soon," Bauer said as he stared out the window at nothing.

When Shade had seated himself at the piano bench, disdaining the chairs that he did not feel qualified to touch his butt to with sufficient appreciation, Crawford leaned toward him.

"It's a terrible thing that has happened to Alvin, poor man. It's not as uncommon an occurrence as we'd all like it to be, I know," Crawford started, then waved his hand. "What am I saying? You know about that better than I, I'm sure." The involuntary spasms of the sorrowful gaze, the sympathetic condolence of the flimsy accolade, all were the memorized lines of a political actor. Mayor Crawford slipped into each with the ease of a pragmatic Olivier. "These burglars nowadays, Shade — what do you think, are they mostly junkies?"

"There are more burglars who are burglars than burglars who are junkies."

"That sounds very informed. It doesn't matter, I don't suppose. Some river-rat Frogtowner sees an apple pie and a Ming vase in somebody's window and decides he will by God kill for a pastry that size." Crawford looked at Bauer, who squirmed, then chortled professionally. "But this, this is one burglar I want caught in a hurry. And it wouldn't break my heart if it was before he sliced the pie and spooned the vanilla on top. Read me?"

An uncomfortable weight of recognition hit Shade.

"I don't think this was a burglary. I think it was murder, straight up and simple."

"What do you think, Captain Bauer?"

Bauer cocked his head and shrugged.

"It could've been a burglar and Rankin surprised him."

"Not from the evidence," Shade said.

"But it happens all the time, does it not?"

"Sure it does," Bauer said.

"No," Shade said. He leaned forward with his elbows on his knees. "Most murdered people get that way on purpose, not as some freak accident. I'm pretty sure it's no Russian roulette sort of thing either, where you put a pistol to the *back* of your head and squeeze off *two* rounds. Nothing was taken from Rankin's house, and he was whacked while peeking at the tube with someone. Most people, when they surprise a burglar, don't ask what channel they want to watch."

Crawford caught Bauer's eye and jerked a thumbs-up toward Shade.

45

"Good man, Captain," he said, then turned back to Shade. "So you think Alvin Rankin was killed by someone close to him?"

"Yes, sir."

"And since he was a city councilman, maybe it all has something to do with that."

"Seems possible."

"Maybe we could start a little parade, eh, Shade?" When a response was slow in coming the mayor began to stalk about the room, lightly fingering various fine knick-knacks, gesticulating silently. "Sure, we could lead the media and the hearts and minds of all of Saint Bruno on an entertaining little trip through the local loony bin we call politics. That way we could get some bold block type asking who all is involved in the assassination of the black heir apparent. Wouldn't that just be great?"

"It'd be the first parade I ever led, Mayor. Not my line."

Captain Bauer wagged a finger at Shade.

"You know what you sound like? You sound like you miss walkin' a beat, is what you sound like. We still have foot patrol way out at the Mall."

Crawford held his hands in front of himself, a calming gesture.

"No need for that," he said. "We can rise above that."

Crawford walked to the coffee service and poured himself another cup. He did not fill the cup, but gracefully streamed three-quarters of a full load into the thin white receptacle, reducing the risk of graceless spillage.

"I remember it now," Crawford said with an unconvincing snap of his fingers. "Frank Shade, over in the D.A.'s office — you two are related, aren't you?"

"Francois is my brother."

"That explains it. You're the fighter."

"Ex."

"Just so," Crawford said. "How could I forget—you cost me a hundred dollars once."

"Hunh? I don't recall that."

"When you fought that stringbean black out at the Armory, the one who hit like King Kong."

"Foster Broome."

"That's right. Foster Broome, from Trenton or Los Angeles, or somewhere like that."

Shade's estimation of the mayor's shrewdness was in danger of being revised by this sporting revelation. Was he fool enough to have bet him seriously, or just to show faith in a hometown boy?

Shade smiled.

"That's nice, Mayor. Not many backed me outside of Frogtown. And it was pride, not calculation, that had them behind me."

"Oh, I don't want to mislead you, Shade. I'm no knucklehead. I dropped a hundred betting you wouldn't last past the third, and you stumbled your way into, what was it, the fifth?"

"The seventh."

"Whatever. Broome was starting to slip." The mayor smirked as if his contempt was, for people like Shade, an attainment of merit. "You must've been pretty sad yourself, getting your big chance and only lasting seven rounds."

"Not really. It's six and a half rounds longer than most men could've lasted."

"I suppose that's true. It sounds right. But then most men aren't supposed to be professionals at that sort of thing, are they?"

"No, sir," Shade said. He stood and placed the coffee cup on the bench beside him. "But they all act like they *could be* if they just had the spare time, and the guts."

"And, of course, the neurotic need."

"Starting to sound a lot like politics, isn't it, sir?"

"What's the matter, Shade—don't you like politicians?"

"Sure I do. I ever get a mongrel that craps in the kitchen and won't fetch I'm going to name him Politician."

Captain Bauer stood with some effort, exhaling loudly, looking worried.

"I'm goin' to step in right here, gents, and call time."

Crawford raised a hand to halt him.

"Karl, when your assistance is required it will be requested." Crawford sat and raised his cup, his dark eyes above the rim holding steady on Shade. When the cup was returned to the saucer balanced on his knee, he said, "You're a half-assed detective and I'm mayor. We get into a public pissing contest, who do you think the judges will favor?"

"Whoever got them appointed might get a few breaks."

"Oh, come on, what's the big deal?" Bauer said. "So you don't see eye to eye immediately, so what? We can work this out." The big man pointed a thick finger at his subordinate. "Shade, save your salty tongue for family gatherings, hear me? And burglary is certainly a possibility to explain this, so what's it hurt to follow it?"

"Just the headlines."

"Is that so bad?" Crawford asked, suddenly smiling.

Shade, who knew a sinking boat when he was on it, kept silent.

"Mayor," Bauer went on, "Shade and Blanchette will do their jobs. When there's something solid we'll have to go with it, but for now this angle is as promising as any."

"Okay, okay," Crawford said as his finger distractedly picked at lint on his robe. "My only concern is to avoid a lot of crazy speculation on who might or might not've had cause to be a party to Alvin's murder. The I'll-pull-on-my-asshole-

and-print-what-comes-out kind of rumor-mongering guess-work can tear a town apart. It can spawn a multitude of head-high dark clouds for the innocent to walk under, if you know what I mean. That would be vicious and unnecessary."

Shade watched Crawford's face, interpreting facial fluctuations, eyebrow histrionics, and hand signals for any accidental tip-off of sincerity, but found none. He was neither surprised nor terribly disappointed that the mayor's first concern was for his own welfare. That was understandable, even reassuring, for it was easier to deal with a venial professionalism that wore the traditional price tags of power, wealth, and position than with some sincere, but combustible, altruism that sought only total victory or martyrdom.

"Why don't I just get on with it, then," Shade said.

"Fine idea," Bauer said. "First rate." He floated one meaty hand down to Crawford's shoulder and patted him sympathetically. "He's very good at street stuff, Gene. Really. We get a call that some Frogtown free-lancer has hit such-and-such a liquor store and by the time a squad car circles the block, Shade here has divined the perp's route and is sittin' on his stoop waitin' for him."

Crawford warped his mouth into a left-handed smile and raised his chin.

"A suspicious skill for a cop," he said.

"But damn handy," Shade replied. "Sometimes suspicious, but always damn handy."

"This is the truth," Captain Bauer said with a bob of his head.

The door beckoned from an attractive proximity, and Shade, following two curt nods, strode to it and out. He stepped onto an early morning lawn, the grass slicked back with dew, the air thick with natural pomade. He slid on the side of the terraced lawn, breathing deeply, his feet acting as skis on the wet slope to the driveway. He kept his balance all the way down, then leaned on the car hood at the bottom.

Blanchette sat watching him but did not gesture.

Shade found himself wondering if he wouldn't be happier as a Catfish Bar regular, a neighborhood survivor with his own stool and a drink named after him, one who could meet the people he'd known for a lifetime without alien suspicions coming between them. Would his father come by more often, with a fifth of Old Bushmills and his Balabushka cue in the stiff leather case, inviting him along on debilitating but lively weekend romps, if he had not chosen sides?

Blanchette leaned his head out of the car window.

"Come on, Rene. Shake a leg, there, huh?"

When Shade was seated on the passenger's side he said, "How, did you ever wonder if maybe, just maybe, we weren't soldiers for the wrong set of lords?"

The full, stolid face of Blanchette shook, and his lower lip hid the upper.

"No," he said. "Because we're Frogtowners and we know better. We ought to anyhow."

"Glad to hear it."

"I mean, we didn't really have what it took for that other life, you know? Or we'd be there."

"I hope that's not the only reason."

"Plus, plus we know, from knee-high on up, that all the assholes, *all* the assholes don't wear blue."

Shade grimaced, and nodded.

"Lest we forget," Shade said. "We should write that down."

4

The spiteful heat of a summer turned sullen reached Voltaire Street early. Sun-faded blinds flapped up on dusty front windows as "Closed" signs were flipped and brown-bag lunches were stashed beneath countertops by optimists seeking coolness for their tuna fish. Delivery men, customers, and owners had gotten the message that the bad sun sent out and slowed to lessen the punishment that any hint of speed would draw. Summer was the mean season along the river, the air thick as syrup, and the sky a lowdown fog that held in the torture.

One floor above Voltaire, Jewel Cobb sat on the couch back, peering out the window. His hands were scratching beneath opposite pits, fingering the bumps that an odd rash had raised. Down home he'd've figured it to be poison oak, but up here he hadn't a clue. One more thing not to like about cities, Jewel thought. Everything came at you in disguise in this human stew; people wore suits with ties and drove cars with huge stereos but they weren't really rich; women wore shorts where the cloth never showed till it was above the swell of the ass, with little tit socks called tubetops on, but they wouldn't go into the alley with a fella even if he showed 'em a wallet stuffed with cabbage. The only straight-up thing about cities was they looked unfriendly, and they were.

Clothes were an affectation in such weather, so Jewel pranced about the room uncovered. Suze still slept, her head beneath two pillows, snoring in the cave she always dug for her eyes.

Jewel drank a cup of coffee and stood before the mirror mounted on the bedroom door. The reflection was not true, he noticed shrewdly. He was thicker than this looking glass would let on. Bulgier and tighter, much prettier around the face.

His shotgun leaned against the other end of the couch and Jewel whisked it up. It was a twelve-gauge pump with a midget barrel and a chopped stock. Duncan had given it to him the night before when he dropped him off.

Me an' this, we're gonna *do it* today, Jewel thought. He faced the mirror again. Wish I had a camera, one of those sixty-second brands. He spread his legs, then bent forward slightly to flex his thighs, sucked tight on his gut, and gripped the shotgun in a squeeze that ballooned his biceps.

It'd be a damn *pleasure* to get killed by that guy there in the mirror. That is, compared to *some* who you could get shot by. Damn straight.

But, Jewel reflected as he lay the shotgun on the dressertop, niggers were sly and crafty, with fancy pistols in their belts and razor blades in the tips of their sneakers. Have to be careful. Watch 'em close.

But no sweat, cuz.

Suze slept in an old red football jersey with the sleeves cut out. Her skin was so pale that Jewel found merely looking at it to be nasty. It was like she never went outside, the sun never caught her at her work, 'cause her work was all in pillowed rooms with the curtains drawn. She was a country girl with just one real talent, but it was the one that travels well and is appreciated around the world.

The bed shifted as Jewel sat on the edge. Suze's body was curled like a hook, and he began to lightly float his fingers around the place where the worm would go. With his other hand he stroked her rump.

She swatted at him, then turned over.

He tried again.

The pillows flew from Suze's face. She raised her upper body and rested on her elbows, blinking at him.

"I am tryin' to sleep, Jewel."

"I was just gonna wake you up sweet, is all."

"What's sweet is sleep."

"There's sweet and there's *sweet*," Jewel said. "Anyhow, I'll be busy later. Won't be home."

He began to force his fingertips into her, but it was like stretching rubber and he wasn't sure he was on the right trail. She lifted his hand.

"That hurts."

Jewel grew sheepish, then a little bit angry that she was making him feel bad for going after his own girl. That's supposed to be settled, that you get *that* when you want it.

"We never done nothin' last night," he said.

"You were too drunk."

"And yesterday was too hot."

Suze rubbed her eyes and yawned, then fell back on the bed.

"Oh, baby," she said. "Your hair is a mess."

"I can't find my comb—you got it?"

"Come here, baby," she said. She took his head into her arms. He leaned into her embrace.

Then he found himself remembering Duncan's instructions.

Now listen to me. Wait at the mouth of the alley with the shotgun in the trash cans there, hear me, cuz? Then all you gotta do is this, and it's not much.

Then he remembered Suze and bent to her neck.

"You a natural rooster, ain't you, baby? You see that sun and you got to rise with it, don't you, lover?"

Now he's a big buck with a crippled right foot, so he'll be limpin' when you see him.

"Sure. The crack of dawn is askin' for it in my book."

Somehow Jewel's body was not following his mind's command and things were not happening right.

"I know what you want," Suze said. She sat all the way up and pushed him over, then crouched to him and took him in her mouth.

This cat dresses nice, he really does, with big red ties and diamond clips, and he drives a maroon LTD with all kind of Afro gadgetry hangin' off it. Can't miss him. He owns the theater there, and he shows up at five. Every day.

"Baby?"

Jewel started, then looked down at Suze.

"Baby," she said. "What's the matter?"

"Nothin'."

"I know better. This ain't like you."

She giggled.

He won't know you. None of them will know you. You pull the shotgun when he gets out of the car. He probably won't even look at you. And if he does, he never saw you before.

"I think I'll go get me some eats," Jewel said, then pushed up from the bed.

"What? What?" Suze's mouth dropped and her face

scrunched unpleasantly. "Not now. Not now you don't, buster."

"Shut your face."

"It ain't right," she said. "I was sleepin'. Before you started on me I was sleepin'. Now I'm started I ain't goin' to be able to sleep." Suze swung out of bed and followed Jewel while he rounded up his clothes. "You ain't goin' nowhere under these circumstances."

He'll walk right past the alley and you'll be hidden pretty good. The blast will shake people up. They'll be runnin' every which way, so you step up close and spread his head out real good. We got to be sure.

"I'm not in the mood," Jewel said. "I got to be in more of a mood."

"Jew-el! For God's sake—I was sleepin'."

"So go back to sleep! It's all you got to do anyhow."

"Well," Suze said, then collapsed her shoulders in surrender. "I mean, praise the Lord, Jew-el."

She grabbed her clothes off the bedpost and went to the bathroom, slamming the door as a final comment.

Immediately admitting that he was no hungrier for food than he'd been for Suze, Jewel dropped his shirt and jeans back to the floor and slumped onto the couch. He pulled his guitar out from beneath the high-legged couch and began to strum an approximate rendition of "Mama Tried." As he played he could see the sidewalk across the street, a sidewalk clotted with strangers doing business, a street he didn't like. Creepy fuckin' Frogs, anyhow.

It's a piece of cake, if you keep cool.

Jewel jerked upright, then flipped the guitar across the room, snapping the E string on the dresser edge. He put his head in his hands and growled.

And you'll keep cool, right, cuz?

55

5

Pete Ledoux sat on the hood of his black Pinto in the shadows of the line of trees that surrounded the graveled parking lot of the Catfish Bar, using his keys to chisel at splatters of guano deposited on his car by a rare bird that shit cement and seemed to follow him around. Occasionally he looked across the lot, foul with white dust and heat shimmers, toward Lafitte Street. He was waiting for Steve Roque, and that meant that he could not become impatient and leave. Roque had said wait, and Ledoux had no choice but to do so.

The sidewalk on this stretch of Lafitte, even before noon, was rich with rod-and-reel luggers in rubber boots sneaking toward a favorite slough where a dry stump overlooked a bullhead hole; double-wide women with surplus neck who squeezed grocery bags to their chests; and diddy-bop strutters in Foster Grants who acknowledged one another with terse chin gestures. Ledoux watched as if Frogtown, the version of it that he'd always known, was on the verge of disappearing. The area had not been totally French since Lewis and Clark had partied down here prior to their famous trip, and even when Ledoux had been born the Frogs had been equaled in number by rogue Germans, ambitious Irish, and hillbilly trash. It was this new influx of wetbacks that troubled him. Those people stank the streets up with peppery smells and burned beans, and they didn't understand who was boss. If native Frogtowners didn't snap out of their soft slumber they'd wake soon to find they lived on Pancho Villa Boulevard. He was sure of that.

When Roque arrived it was on foot. He stood at the corner of the bar building and raised a hand toward Ledoux. Ledoux crossed the parking lot and joined him beneath the big sign with a blue catfish on it that swung above the door.

A bouncy kid was swaggering down the walk. He was summer brown and wore a coffee-stained dago T-shirt, dress slacks, and slick shoes with the de rigueur horseshoe taps that sparked as he walked, as if his strut were a blade and the street a perpetual whetstone. When he was even with the two men he picked Ledoux to make eye contact with.

Ledoux returned the gaze, superior and cool.

The kid shrugged and looked away, then glared back.

"Hey, punk," Ledoux said sharply, "I don't want to be your friend. Keep walkin'."

"Fuck you," the kid said, then looked over his shoulder.

Ledoux leaned toward him and the kid flashed a couple of running steps, then slowed to a walk when he saw he wasn't being seriously chased.

"I don't think I can put up with it," Ledoux said.

"Shouldn't have to," Roque said. "That's my opinion."

Steve Roque was built in the style of the local French: about five-ten, with a thick-boned frame, filled out by two hundred pounds of unpretentious, but useful, bulk. So many Frog-towners were of this body type that it was referred to as "Froggy." But Roque sidestepped stereotyping by being bald, with a long gray rough of hair on the sides. He wore a black Ban-Lon shirt, white slacks, and white shoes.

Roque jerked his thumb at the door.

"I heard there's a cool spot in this town; could be it's in here."

Froggy Russ Poncelet, the day bartender, a friend to many and enemy to none, was busy behind the bar dropping cans of beer into the floor coolers. He looked up as Roque and Ledoux entered.

"Tip's in back," he said.

"Hard worker, that Tip," Roque replied.

"How do you like this heat?" Poncelet asked.

"Not much. It's yours for a cheeseburger."

They took a table in the back, far removed from the other customers. The Catfish drew a decent lunch business but it was still too early for the legitimately hungry to appear, so the few tables of customers were made up of unemployed, but entrepreneurial, young men, as well as the diurnal conventions of phlegmatic tipplers.

Roque peeled a thin cigar and lit it. As he inhaled, he looked over the room and received waves from two of the tables. Not familiar waves, but respectful acknowledgments of his presence. He nodded back.

Less relaxed than Roque, Ledoux spent considerably more time inspecting the clientele before hunching forward and saying, "I saw the papers this morning. Man, are they confused."

"Of course they are," Roque said. "What'd you expect?" His brown eyes were not cold, but warm with malice and bright with confidence. "They might unravel it, but not in time to change much. That is, if *you* can hold *your* end up."

Poncelet approached the table, drying his hands on the untucked portion of his white T-shirt.

"What'll it be, fellas? Something to drink, or you want some chow?"

"How about air conditioning?" Roque asked. To emphasize his request he scraped a finger across his forehead, then flicked sweat to the floor.

"We don't carry it," Poncelet said.

"How much is Tippy kickin' to the building inspector, huh? 'Cause this is unsafe heat."

"Is that supposed to be in the nature of *news* to me?"

Roque grunted.

"No, I guess not. You hungry?" he asked Ledoux.

"Nah. I'll just have a Stag with a glass."

"Merci," Poncelet said. "And you, Steve?"

"I want to eat," Roque said. "I'll have a tall glass of ice water and some chicken stew."

"Coq au vin, you mean."

"Right. Chicken stew with a sneer. You sound like my grandmother."

"Look like her, too," Poncelet said, then returned to the bar.

"He's a smart-ass," Roque said.

"But a likable one."

"Most of them are — up to a point."

The men sat in silence until Poncelet returned with their orders, then left them.

"So — Crane had it in him, hunh," Ledoux said. "I wasn't sure. I didn't think he would for sure."

"Well, he did," Roque said. "Took some convincin'. Had

to mention Tony Duquette and Ding-Ding Stengel a couple of times. Had to remind him about Curly Boone, and how his house burned down around his ears that time when *he* couldn't pay up. And he owed me less than *you* do, I said to Crane."

"And Teejay Crane's a nigger, too. Boone at least was white."

Roque grunted, then shook his head.

"That doesn't mean a thing." Roque spooned a piece of chicken from the bowl, then took it in his fingers and sucked the meat from the bone. "Payin' what you owe is all that counts."

Ledoux's eyes narrowed as he looked away. It couldn't be true, what Roque said, about black or white not making a difference.

"Why'd you bring up Duquette and Stengel? Ain't I takin' care of business good enough for you?"

"Sure you are. I think. You keep tellin' me you are, anyhow. But no sense in mentionin' a guy like *you* to Crane, who was nervous and no idiot, you know. I think he could see how he'd be extra weight once he'd done the big dance with Rankin." Roque nodded, then sipped some ice water. "I think he'd done this sort of thing once before."

After draining half a glass of Stag Ledoux began to stroke his chin reflectively.

"It's nice," he said. "The way it fits together is nice. Crane thinks his dirty movie racket, there, is solvent again, and he don't have to worry no more about his kids and stuff. That was ruinin' his days, I'll betcha, wonderin' what closet was goin' to spring open full of Frogs with bad intentions."

"I think maybe you're right," Roque said. "He knew he was in a spot. If Rankin hadn't've started thinkin' he could be cute with me like he did, Crane would've tried to swim to New

Orleans some time back. Me, though, I always plan for the future."

Ledoux, flush with the pleasures of conspiracy, began to smile serenely.

"You know, if Sundown Phillips figures out his main man got whacked by Crane, why Crane would die bad, mon ami. A lot worse than we're goin' to do him."

Roque laughed, a steel-on-cement rumble.

"Must be goin' to parochial school that made us so thoughtful."

"I always went to public."

"Well, me too. After the third grade."

The bowl of stew was not empty but Roque shoved it to the middle of the table. Ledoux, with a beer growling on an empty stomach, began to appraise an onion quarter and a piece of chicken that were left over.

"Yeah," Roque said, "if Rankin hadn't've gotten the not-so-bright idea that his committee, there, the Bids Committee, could throw us over for his own people, Phillips Construction, why, a whole lot of peace never would've got disturbed."

"It always happens. A guy needs you, so you help him, then he doesn't need you so much anymore, mon ami, 'cause you've been *so* much help, and then it's out to the shithouse with you." Ledoux shook his head at the disappointing nature of human intercourse. "You were makin' each other rich, but he wanted more — am I right?"

"Well, there's another thing here." Roque lifted his powerful shoulders and turned his hands out. "One — I really want to be the man who builds the Music Center. It's none of your business why, but I do. Leave it at that. Two — I think Phillips would've done less for him over the long run anyhow, but he didn't want to see that."

61

"You got a point there," Ledoux said, then unleashed his hand and let it snatch up the onion quarter and chicken part.

Roque's hand sprang forward and grabbed Ledoux by the wrist.

"Put that back!" he said.

"What?"

"Put it back! You deaf or something?"

Roque shook Ledoux's preying hand until the food splashed back in the bowl.

Ledoux wiped his released hand on a napkin.

"What's the fuckin' deal?" he asked.

"You don't take my food, that's what. That's *my* food. If I wanted you to take it I'd tell you to take it."

"You were done."

Roque leaned forward, scooting the table in on Ledoux.

"You hungry, Pete? You said you weren't hungry, but if you are I'll get you a bowl of stew and you can eat it with your own spoon and everything."

After a sip of beer Ledoux shook his head.

"Ever since I was a kid," Roque said, "I haven't liked that. People nibbling at *my* food, I don't like it."

"It was just goin' to be wasted. I didn't see the point in wastin' it when I'm just a little bit hungry."

"If I want to waste it, then I waste it. It's mine."

"Forget it," Ledoux said. He didn't know where to look, what to put his eyes on. He finished his beer and stood. "I better go get this peckerwood and his cousin in gear for us."

"Don't go away mad, Pete. If you're hungry — eat. I'll buy."

"I'm not fuckin' hungry!"

As Ledoux stared at Roque's hard face he heard steps coming up from behind. He felt a hand clap him on the back.

"How's it goin', Pete?" Tip Shade asked.

"Okay."

"Hemorrhoids botherin' you, or are you on your way out?" Tip sat down at the table and nodded at Roque.

"He's decidin' whether or not to eat," Roque said.

"No I ain't." Ledoux wiggled a hand in front of his zipper. "I'm goin' to go shed a tear for Ireland, that's what. Then I got business."

"Good enough," Roque said.

"What's this about pissin' on Ireland?" asked Thomas Patrick Shade, a tricultural man with dangerous pride in the two homelands he'd never seen.

"It's just an expression," Ledoux said. Nods of agreement appeared all around and Ledoux smiled. "Besides — who you think you're kiddin' — you're a Frog."

"When I want to be, I am," Tip said. "Every March I'm Irish."

Ledoux walked away, and as he sighted in on the john he heard Tip ask: "Say, what about old Alvin Rankin, there, Steve. That'll shake Pan Fry up, won't it?"

"I would guess it would," Roque said. "But as long as they only kill each other, who can gripe? Not you, not me. That's what I got to ask — who's goin' to be upset?"

6

In the heart of Frogtown, or Old French Town, as the historical markers labeled it, the streets were burnt-orange cobblestone, and brick row houses were built so that the front doors opened onto traffic instead of sidewalks. There were handmade signs for Pierre's Shoes, Secondhand and New, Jacqueline's Herbs and Spices, and at the corner of the line of row houses on Lafitte and Perry, Ma Blanqui's Pool House.

The downstairs of the house had two pool tables in what had once been the parlor and one in the former dining room. In the rear was a small kitchen, a bedroom, and a large closet without a door on it. Monique Blanqui Shade sat in the closet on a high stool from which she kept an eye on the tables. A large Dr Pepper cooler served as a counter and gave her storage space for the extras she sold.

The upstairs was a separate apartment although the door that connected it to the downstairs had no lock on it. That had never been a problem, for Rene Shade lived in the upper half. He lived there partly because he believed, despite considerable contrary evidence, that his mother might need his protection in this neighborhood, but primarily because it was cheap.

On the morning following his meeting with Mayor Crawford, Shade woke sometime before noon but could not pull himself from bed. The apartment was dark and he looked around the room, his familiarity with its accoutrements causing him to overlook the fistful of trophies on a bookcase, the Brueghel reproductions on the wall, and the clothing strewn across the floor. He found himself staring at a cooing pigeon on the window ledge, a ledge well used by pigeons; a pigeon he could not hush by voice command alone. He considered throwing something that would rattle the window and panic the bird, then passed on such a serious test of his aim so early in the day.

He pulled a pillow over his eyes and tried to sleep.

Sometime later, caught in the lucid but immobile state where the subconscious rambles and the conscious listens, Shade became aware of wet blossoms sprouting from his body. The damp tulips unfolded on his neck, his belly, and then on ground where sweet blossoms live dangerously. His hand began to follow the pattern of moist horticulture and finally grasped a bud just planted but beginning to spread.

"Got me," a voice like a blue saxophone said.

Slowly Shade sat up, a few strands of Nicole Webb's hair wound between his fingers.

"What round is it?" he said.

Nicole draped her arms around his neck.

"The first," she said. "And you're winning."

"Just a minute," Shade said. He rolled out of bed and clumsily walked to the bathroom. He bent over the sink to

65

splash water on his face, then crouched to the faucet and irrigated the potato field that his mouth had become.

Nicole, a rare good fortune for a post-twenties single man in that she was mature but not cautious, and confident but not aloof, leaned against the doorjamb.

"You're not wearing the underwear I bought you," she said. "You must not like it."

Shade rubbed his face with a towel.

"See a beach?" he asked. "Where's the sand?"

"They're bikini briefs," Nicole said. "That just means sexy underwear."

"I thought naked was sexy."

"Well, it is. But sexy comes in stages."

Nicole wore cutoff jeans, with stylish unravelings that formed slits along the seams, and a black T-shirt that advertised Sister Kettle's Cafe. The benefits of racquetball and modest weight training gave her arms a fetching versatility of attitude. Black hair, with traces of red when in sunny silhouette, was tucked in a bun. Her waist was thin, her breasts indisputably there, although not garish, all set atop a length of leg that was extravagant and winning.

Shade tossed the towel into the tub, then put his arm around Nicole, and whispered, "I have something to show you."

They started toward the bed, the tangling energies of their affections making for awkward strides.

"I hope it's something I've seen before," Nicole said.

As the sun began to ruin the day with heat, Nicole traced her fingers over Shade's variety of acquired imperfections. There were tiny pale nicks above both eyes, evidence of his former livelihood, and a long gash beneath his chin, put there by the dangerous mix of a too-large bicycle, a small boy, and a hill of challenging steepness. Behind his left shoulder there was a puckered horseshoe, hung there by the doting mother of a busted drug dealer and the avenging end of a broken ketchup bottle.

Shade looked up at Nicole, then rolled over.

"How'd you get in here, anyway?" he asked.

"I came through from downstairs."

"Hunh." Shade stood and began to gather his clothes. "Ma let you up, or did you sneak?"

"We had a cup of coffee, then I came up."

"She never lets anybody come up those stairs. You start up those stairs, usually she hits you."

"She likes me," Nicole said with a grin. "And I don't have a key to the other door."

In his pants now, Shade walked to the refrigerator and pulled out a can of juice. He popped the top, drank, then wiped his mouth.

"That ought to tell you something," he said.

"What ought to tell me something?"

"That you don't have a key."

Groaning, Nicole twisted away from Shade and smirked at the opposite wall.

Shade went on: "You don't have a key because I've never given you one. You didn't call or anything before you came over, you just showed up. That's why I don't give out keys."

"Ho, ho," Nicole said. She slid into her shorts, then turned her T-shirt right side out, hunching away from Shade. "I've been presumptuous. There are crowds clamoring for your house key, and I circumvent your rationing plan by coming in the door that doesn't lock."

"You don't have the right to just come in anytime you want, Nicole."

Nicole pulled her shirt on, then cocked her head and smiled sarcastically.

"Your privacy wasn't so precious an hour ago. You could've sent me packing right at the start."

Bent over to tie his shoes, Shade said, "I guess I was still groggy."

Nicole laughed, though it wasn't the sweetest laugh in her repertoire.

"You could've told me before you fucked me."

"Before *I* fucked *you?* You mean before *we* fucked, don't you?"

"That's a pretty modern concept for you, Rene."

Shade's face drained of personality, and a dull commonness became his expression.

"Yeah," he said. "I can also use a telephone, plug in a toaster, identify airplanes — stuff like that."

As she wagged her head, and dazedly smiled at this intrusion of romantic debate, Nicole searched the floor for the panties that had been furiously abandoned earlier, when privacy had been a secondary desire.

In the small kitchen, Shade turned the fire on beneath a kettle of water, then put a filter in the coffee pot and scooped in a pile of Yuban. He set two cups on the counter, then turned to Nicole.

"This is crazy," he said. "I don't even mind, really. I don't know why I barked at you. A hard-learned habit, I guess."

Spotting the wad of her red panties on the top shelf of the bookcase, Nicole did not respond.

"You want a key?" Shade asked. "You want a key, you should have a key. I'm not pokin' anybody else, anyway."

"Poking?" Nicole said, the panties now in her hand. "Is that what you're doing? You're *poking* me? Is that what you tell people?"

"Ah, shit," Shade said. He concentrated on watching the kettle not boil. "It's just an expression. A bad one, maybe."

"*Maybe?*"

Nicole rolled the panties tight, then squeezed them into the watchpocket of her cutoffs. She walked to the back door and opened it. The river roiled just beyond the railroad tracks and formed the background for her dramatic pose in the doorway.

"You have some things to think about," she said. "Me, too."

"You want a key, you can have a key."

"Rene," she said, a sonorous rebuke in her intonation. "That's not it. This is *not* about a key."

"Oh, I see," Shade said. He raised the now boiling water and poured it into the steeping chamber of the coffee pot.

"I'll get a copy knocked off over at the hardware store and leave it in your mailbox for you."

Nicole shrugged, looked down, then up.

"If you really want to," she said.

"I do."

She eased inside then, and pulled the door closed behind her.

"Today?"

7

Jewel Cobb had long conjured scenarios of murder during his nighttime fantasies, but when he was finally prepared to make the big step up in his midnight world, he found himself in a premature nocturne, the sun still walking its watchful beat, and the sidewalks becoming hectic as five o'clock neared.

He dripped potato chips as he slouched in the front of an alley between three stories of soot-bricked warehouse and two stories of Teejay Crane's retrospectively opulent theater, his hand on a string between a Kitty Clover bag and the vicinity of his mouth. There were glass chunks on the asphalt and he pushed at them with his boots until they crunched and gave way. A quart of Falstaff beer in a paper bag sat near his feet, and he occasionally crouched to it for a swig.

The shotgun was in the second of four trash cans outside the fire exit of the theater. He'd brought it in a grocery sack, the piece broken into two components, both the barrel and the stock shortened by a hacksaw. He'd huddled over the trash can like a retching drunk while he reassembled the shotgun, loaded it, then eased it along the edge of the garbage, careful not to clog the barrel, stock up for easy grabbing.

The instructions Duncan and Ledoux had given him played over and over in his mind. In the alley, wait, whack him, head shot, drop the piece and walk down Seventh Street, turn left, and escape will be waiting there in a car. Jewel had it all memorized but that failed to plump up his confidence.

The chips were all gone. He kicked at the empty bag, then squatted to the Falstaff.

He was within twenty feet of Seventh Street but no one paid much attention to him. He blended into the surroundings, just another down-and-outer, although younger than most, and somewhat of a pacesetter sartorially. Whenever there was accidental eye contact he dropped his head and began to rock it on his neck as if shaking off one of those famous drinking companions who are mammoth and pink but very rarely seen by more than one drunken witness.

He was telling time by the clock in the window of Shevlin's Fair Deal Pawnshop and Rentals across the street. Crane was said to be as predictable as misery and Jewel could see that he was due in five minutes.

All he could do was wait, and watch. He did not like the area. It was like all the cracked-shingle scruffy houses he'd ever lived in, but pushed all together in one spot, then stacked up to make a city.

The marquee of the theater announced that *Candy and the Eighth Dwarf* was "Now Playing." Jewel wondered what it was that cities put over on folks that made them want to spend money to watch strangers have real good times.

At almost straight-up five a wino with a bald head laced by what looked like scuff marks, and with fermenting clothes and white gloves, pulled out of the ambling herd on Seventh and into the alley. He carried a large grocery bag that clearly contained a gallon-sized bottle.

Jewel looked down as the wino passed, his nose wrinkling in disgust. He looked up in time to see his visitor approach the trash cans.

"Get out of there," Jewel said evenly, then sprang to his feet. "Hey, you! Get out of there!"

The wino looked at him with sleepy eyes.

"Grub your chow somewhere else," Jewel said. "Go find your own trash cans."

"But these *are* mine," the wino said in the tone of a shy boy being picked on by his teacher. "They been mine ever since Wally the Hog left. That made 'em mine. Let's see, that would be when the men went up and tracked mud on the moon. Around then. They got money for doin' it, I'd bet. It was the cleanest place in the world before they went and did that."

After glancing out to the street and not seeing Teejay Crane's maroon LTD, Jewel said, "It might still be. That's quite a while back anyhow."

"Wally the Hog had 'em longer, but he died. He never left, like I said. He died."

"I'll give 'em back to you tomorrow."

"I don't know nothin' about it, you see. My last cough drop says it was his heart. All them butts he was always pickin' up." The wino pinched two gloved fingers to his throat and gobbled, then began walking in reverse. "He thought it was just his good luck to find 'em, and it was, too, till they killed him." He stopped and squinted at Jewel. "I heard he smoked a halfie after a Chinaman tossed it—now you *know* that *can't* be good for you."

Jewel glanced down the alley, then back to the street.

"I warned him more times than I've shit," the wino testified.

"Sure," Jewel said. "I been knowin' better than that my whole life."

"Well," the wino said with a nod, "told the police 'bout it, too."

"You what?" Jewel said. He advanced on the wino, jerked him by the shoulders and spun him about, then booted his ass. "Why you old snitch — get the fuck out of here."

The wino, after an initial burst of rapid steps, settled into a measured wobble, his immediate future hugged protectively to his chest, not even glancing back over his shoulder with concern.

Somewhat irritated by his inability to provoke paralyzing fear, even in bums with spoonable brains, Jewel watched until the wino was fifty feet down the alley. He'd seen a movie once where it turned out even Comanches wouldn't tweak the noses of unknown fates by spearing outright crazies. He got the point of it, now, and it didn't have anything at all to do with having sung too many old Baptist hymns.

Jewel moved forward and began to hover on the edge of the sidewalk. The masquerade of being an aimless bum he only occasionally remembered. His eyes searched every passing car and he tensed up at the sight of every large black man who was better dressed than he was. He should've asked more questions, he saw that now. *He's a big buck who dresses nice.* A multitude of victims filled the sidewalks. Show me a big buck who *don't* dress nice, hunh? If I see one I'll shoot him, 'cause he's gotta be in with the laws.

The minutes crawled by like daddy time had been kneecapped. The clock in Shevlin's window now read nine after five.

Jewel began to pace. He kept looking back to the second trash can where just a sliver of the stock showed above the garbage. Maybe two times a year the sucker's late, and this had to be one of them. A horrible thought struck Jewel: maybe he got a ride, maybe the maroon LTD got a flat and he got a ride and I won't have no way of knowin' him. Or maybe he'd fix it himself. Maybe he's the kind of sensible nigger who'd put his hundred-dollar shoes on the floorboards and his coat on the front seat and bend down to fix the flat himself, barefoot.

Jesus.

And Cuz and the Frog might not understand the situation and leave or something.

An argument began to echo down the narrow-bricked, litter-decorated alley. Jewel turned around and saw the wino of his acquaintance being the reluctant dancer in a three-person variation of the Seventh Street Waltz. Slurred curses dribbled through the air, and the wino curled over his bottle while two erect hoofers took turns kicking his back.

What a bunch of noisy bums, Jewel thought. How can people live that way?

One of the team-oriented bums said something to the prone, stingy brother of the grape. It had to do with sharing, just like the rest of us, just like last night when I had the good day.

"Pint!" the wino screamed as he curled more tightly around his gallon of red. "Pints are silly!"

The chastening two-step began again and for the briefest of seconds Jewel thought about going down there and putting a stop to it. But it's just their ways, he thought, and anyway they'll end up slobberin' all over each other with dumb smiles on their faces once he's had enough boots to the spine. Besides, this is America — that means you can get however much you can grab, but keepin' it's your own damn problem.

So accustomed to disappointment did Jewel's eye for color become that when the maroon LTD passed in front of him he did not recognize it until the car was halfway down the block. He jerked around and looked at the trash can, then stepped out onto the sidewalk to watch the car park.

The car pulled to the curb on the theater side of the street, about fifty parking spaces down, nearly half a block away.

The driver's door didn't open.

Jewel checked the clock and saw that he was nearly twenty minutes late, and still Crane had not emerged from the long-anticipated maroon background.

What's he doin' in there, anyway?

Jewel's foot nudged the empty Falstaff bottle, then he looked down and kicked at it. A glancing blow pushed the brown-bagged bottle onto its side where it pinwheeled, then came to rest in a divot in the asphalt.

When he looked up his stomach flopped like a prizewinning bass, and his hands felt weak. Teejay Crane was on the sidewalk, limping right into Jewel's showdown midnight.

Jewel scooted to the trash can, second one in, and lifted his crime partner, then flicked the safety off. He felt as though he were floating back to the sidewalk. He leaned against the wall of the theater, using his body to shield the shotgun.

When Crane was twenty car lengths away a dark-skinned woman in blue sneakers and a shawl with leopard spots on it said something to him and he stopped.

He couldn't hear what they said, but Jewel saw that what he'd been told was true. Crane was *big,* and dressed real nice, with a red velvet pimp jacket on that looked like it would've took a three-day convention of railroad men to pay for. Fuckin' pimps.

Crane kept smiling at the woman and saying things that caused both their torsos to shudder and their mouths to stretch.

Come on, man, Jewel thought as he tapped the sawed-off against the back of his leg. Give her the brush, huh? She ain't so such a much.

Crane did not move, but stood there working on the feline-clad woman as if he wanted election and she were a crowd. His hands went up, then out, and sometimes they patted her on the shoulder. Her leopard leaped as she squealed happily, her knees buckling, then springing her back to full height.

Time was changing things. Jewel didn't know how long Cuz and the Frog would wait but quittin' time was long overdue. He thought about going down the sidewalk and taking Crane off right there. He knew that it was strictly uh-uh to do that, but circumstances weren't dovetailing with his plans.

He continued to watch, and wait, then a trembling urge for the spectacular propelled him onto the sidewalk toward Crane. He swaggered straight down the middle of the side-walk, being cagey with the shotgun at first, then, surrendering to the flamboyance that he had long coveted, he raised it in his right hand and began to point it as if it were a pistol.

Loafers became ambulant, even speedy, as Jewel approached, and an army of snazzily dressed strangers got out of his path. Several gasped and invoked the deity, while a shrewd etiquette caused others to look away.

When Jewel had closed to within a Cadillac of Crane, the woman put her hand to her mouth and stutter-stepped backward.

"Oh, Mr. Crane," she said. "What's this?"

The barrel of the shotgun, shortened to provide a wider

shot pattern and nastier look, was trained on the slightly gray head of Teejay Crane.

Crane followed the woman backward, as if the shotgun were aimed at him by accident and if he moved it would sight on something else. But when he moved the muzzle followed, and suddenly his heavy shoulders slumped. He looked at his feet and raised his hands as though the brilliant whiteness of his palms would save him.

"I ain't even surprised," Crane said dully. "I guess I knew it."

When Jewel stepped forward Crane decided to pop-quiz fate, and tried to limp away more cunningly than buckshot could follow, but when he made his first zig he was ripped high in the shoulder by the opening blast. He crumpled in a spin, once more facing Jewel.

Jewel had not really heard the shot, but he'd sort of felt it jangling up his arm. He pumped another shell into the chamber. There was blood on the sidewalk, and a little fountain of it sprayed from Crane. People disappeared from the street. He looked down at Crane, whose eyes had narrowed, his lips tightening with disappointment, as if some small thing had displeased him.

With the next shot Jewel turned the man's forehead inside out. He quickly whirled in a tight-pivoting circle.

"I ain't kiddin'!" he shrieked. He could hear his voice, the echo of it seeming to linger. Or maybe he had repeated his cry.

With the muzzle pointed down he started toward the corner of Benton Street, but several men began to move in a storefront there and one of them held his hands inside his jacket.

"No, you don't," Jewel said, backing up. "I can't believe that."

He looked up the street and down, then spun once more,

dropped the shotgun, and started to run back the way he'd come. At first it was a calculated jog, his path clear as his dreams, but then he overshot the alley. He wanted to turn around because that alley was the only other way to the escape car. But people were already standing up from between parked cars and someone shouted encouragement for him to be killed.

Then he started running with nothing held back, entering blocks he'd never seen before. Blocks full of people who he was certain would not like him even if they'd known him from the cradle.

Jewel's brain began to ricochet off vague sayings and childish knowledge.

Some Indians can run a hundred miles a day. In the desert, with meat hung from their belts.

The new sidewalks of people did not part for him and he shoved his way through without articulate comment. He was lost, and running was becoming harder. His breathing was ragged and his feet did not land where he aimed them. His legs felt full of rips.

A man can outrun a horse for the first forty yards. That's proven. The first forty yards belong to the man, but what about after that? Please! What about it?

Oh, please?

8

Pete Ledoux, a man with a vast experience of ugliness, sat behind the steering wheel of a yellow VW bug and watched people pour toward Seventh Street like a fistful of BBs down a funnel. He knew that that meant it had happened, but enough time had passed that fright had eased and curiosity taken over. Sirens already sounded their luring wail.

Ledoux turned to Duncan Cobb who sat in the back seat.

"Keep the piece hidden," he said. "Something fucked up."

The pressures of the day were reflected by the bellicose sag of Duncan's pale, fleshy face.

"That would be Jewel," he said of his cousin. "If it's fucked up, it must be Jewel."

"He might be the one who fucked up, but we're the ones with a problem."

Ledoux started the car, grimacing at the low-rent rattle of the engine.

"Couldn't you've gotten anything else?" he asked as he pulled into traffic. "I mean, really."

"You wanted something that wouldn't be too hot," Duncan said. "The owner of this car is on vacation for five days."

"How can you know that?"

" 'Cause he's a friend of mine."

"You stole it from your friend?"

"Hey, it's safe, Pete. It's safe, and safe is what you wanted."

"Okay," Ledoux said with a shrug. "But I *never* go on vacation, *buddy.*"

The traffic on Benton Street was slow and civilized until it got to Seventh Street, but there many drivers stared at the fattening crowd, then pulled to the curb when the fear that they were missing a gruesome event of historical importance became too strong.

The yellow bug made a U-turn at Seventh, then cruised back down Benton.

"He ain't goin' to make it," Ledoux said. "Would he shoot it out, do you think? Or lay down and wait to be popped?"

"Maybe Crane got *him* first." Duncan began to rub at his thick neck, then exercised his head until his neck crackled. "I don't know what he'd do. How could I know? If he ran, he doesn't know his way around. If he runs he'll get lost."

"He gets caught, we're the ones who're lost. We got to find the dumb peckerwood."

"We'll find him."

After a meaningful glance over his shoulder, Ledoux said, "We better. He was your gimmick, mon ami."

"You don't need to tell me that, man."

"I just want to keep it straight. I got a good head for rememberin' who fucked up."

"That's called survival."

"You ain't tellin' me a thing, mon ami."

They cruised the neighborhood, and squeezed down alleys, searching for Jewel with no luck. Ledoux called it off, and decided to go on with things.

He drove through town, passing the thin, hungry-looking houses, the vulgarly named taverns, and weed-filled lots that were the south side's counterpart to the north side's Frogtown. It had not always been wise for Frogtowners to sightsee in this district, but over the years Ledoux had managed to learn his way around in it. As in all of the old parts of town, the river was the dominant feature here, and if you kept it in sight you could not become seriously doubtful of your whereabouts.

"I thought we had it all dicked out so smooth," Ledoux said, then looked at Duncan in the rearview mirror.

Duncan did not reply.

"Mon Dieu," Ledoux said and pulled to the side of the road. "Get in the front seat, huh? It looks sort of odd, you sittin' back there when the front seat is empty."

"Sure."

When Duncan had shifted his bulk from back to front, Ledoux headed out of town on South River Road.

The edge of town was the point at which houses became more rare, but larger and newer, with lawns kept cleaner than a Presbyterian retreat and long sleek driveways that acknowledged the street only by affecting wrought-iron gates with cherub locks. Ledoux drove past these upscale snubs until River Road crossed the railroad tracks and became a white rock lane.

The lane curved and dipped deep into the lush tangle of trees, weeds, and mud that bordered the river. The VW bounced through weeds that were double its height and around trees that were nearly as thick. Ledoux stalled twice in red-mud gullies but managed to climb out both times.

Soon they came upon Ledoux's black Pinto parked in a small clearing just back of a river bluff. Ledoux slowed enough to look over the car, then, having seen that it had not been tampered with, he drove on. A couple of football fields further on he stopped beneath the remains of a railroad bridge. The breeze bounced off of the black skeletal shape in haunting musical phrases.

He parked near the edge of the bluff, overlooking the wide expanse of strong-flowing rank water. Swirls and eddies marked the treacherous spots in the flow.

Duncan walked to look down the steep bluff, leaning carefully at the edge.

"Is it deep enough here?" he asked.

"It's been dredged," Ledoux said with certainty. "I know this river good. You could drop the Arch in there and just have enough stickin' up to dive off of."

"Hunh." Duncan had the pistol in the front of his waistband. He tapped at it with his fingernails. Offshore and thirty yards downstream there was a large sandbar that seemed handy, but remote. "Should I toss this piece over there, Pete? Or keep it?" He held the pistol up. "That'd be a good place to dump it."

Ledoux had been looking through the car for anything that might have been accidentally dropped. He didn't find anything.

"Did you use it?"

"You know I didn't."

"Then why toss it? That's a Browning Hi-Power. It's got fourteen shots and no serial number. I can't get that many of 'em, peckerwood."

Duncan's face tightened and his slouch straightened indignantly.

"Hey, man, I'm workin' for you and all, but you should know this: pricks don't make friends."

A well-practiced snort of derision honked from Ledoux.

"I don't want friends, you silly shit. Friends — hah! Friends are the ones shoot you twice in the back of the head. Friends snitch you out for the long stretches. Up the joint, you see a guy doin' life you can figure he had one too many friends."

Duncan smirked.

"Let me see. I reckon that's supposed to rattle me, huh? Supposed to sound hardcase and brilliant or something, ain't it?"

"That's what you think, but you don't know, do you?"

After a short smile-and-stare-off between the two men Ledoux returned to the car. He released the parking brake and moved the gearshift to neutral.

"We got to walk back to my car," Ledoux said. "I like to get exercise over with as soon as possible. Let's sink this hunk of junk."

The men walked to the rear of the car so they could shove in unison.

"Maybe we should wait," Duncan said. "You know, until we can put Jewel in there like we wanted."

"Uh-uh," Ledoux said. "That plan is out the window. Just do what I say."

The men leaned into the car and pushed. Once the car started rolling it was easy. The yellow VW staggered over the slick mudbank and slid sideways into the river.

They stood on the bluff and watched. Brown waves lapped at the car doors and the bug began to shake.

"If Jewel was in there we'd be done and home clean," Duncan said sadly.

"Yeah. Only *he* ain't and *we* ain't."

The VW now picked up speed downstream, not sinking, but bobbing like a gargantuan cork.

"Oh, shit!" Ledoux said. "Those fuckin' things don't sink. Lucky damn thing we didn't get the punk. He'd be propped up in there grinnin' at fishermen and skinny-dippers all the way to Baton Rouge."

"Nah," Duncan said. "They sink. I think they sink. But slow."

"It better."

"Maybe I should shoot it, you know. Help it sink."

"Not now."

The car submerged slowly as it drifted with the current. When only the roof and part of the rear window were above water the car nudged into the sandbar and stuck.

"I could blast the windows out if you want."

"No. It beat us. Let it go."

Ledoux stared at the uncooperative vehicle for another moment, then turned and stomped down the lane toward his own car. His face was pursed in serious thought and his feet sank in the mud of the lane.

"Tell me," he said, "has the moon been actin' odd lately, or anything like that?"

"I couldn't say."

"I mean, have you noticed?"

"Can't say that I have," Duncan replied, humoring the older man.

"But you wouldn't anyway, would you? You wouldn't know odd if you saw it."

"I think I might, yeah. If it was real odd."

Ledoux snorted, then sped up.

"Real odd makes the newspapers, peckerwood. For God's sake — it's the *minor* odds you got to train yourself to spot. I learned that the hard way. "

"Not well enough, though," Duncan said with a laugh.

"That," Ledoux said, "will have to be proved."

9

Earlier in the afternoon Shade had been directed to Captain Bauer's office. He knocked on the thick maple, windowless door, then let himself in. The captain was standing in front of the far office window, his hands hanging limply at his sides. Mayor Crawford, dressed in black funereal garb of Italian cut and gemstone worth, sat on the settee with his legs crossed and his hands clasped over the dominant knee.

The cloud of contentment that Nicole's visit had left Shade on evaporated abruptly.

The mayor nodded toward a young dark man of stovepipe build in a three-piece blue pinstripe suit, with a yellow hankie flourish in the breast pocket.

"I don't believe you two need an introduction," he said.

"No, I think not," Shade said, sensing a skillful squeeze play beginning to develop. "How's tricks, Francois?" he said to his younger brother.

"Unsuccessful," Francois replied. "That's why I concentrate on just being good."

The captain turned to look at him, grimaced, then swiveled back to the apparently mesmerizing view outside the window.

The mayor caught Shade's eye and smiled.

"Your brother has caught the Rankin case — isn't that cozy? We like to see good coordination between the police and the D.A.'s office."

"Yes, Mayor," Francois said, hunching forward into the power mode squat. "That's crucial to winning cases."

"Uh, yes," said the mayor with a peaked smile. "Of course." He stood then and walked to the door. "Frank — if I may call you Frank?"

"Please do."

" — has been briefed on the case. You two do whatever it is you do. Share info, or whatever."

"What info?" Shade asked.

"Look, Shade," Mayor Crawford said, "we have files and more files on a cornucopia of burglars, I'm sure. How about starting with *that* information?"

When the mayor had gone, Captain Bauer excused himself with an embarrassed grunt, and left the brothers alone in his office.

Francois stood, smiled nervously, then strode to the massive desk and perched on the edge of it. He ran a long-fingered hand across his thirty-dollar haircut.

"Look," he said. "This is business, blood."

Shade nodded slowly.

"I'm a hundred percent ears."

"Well, what it is is there's beaucoup pitfalls surrounding this case, Rene. I mean, a dude could make one little bitty step wrong here, but it could turn out to be the giantest step he ever took — right or wrong."

Shade looked away, feeling the blood rise in his face. In front of other lawyers or businessmen or women in Parisian attire, Francois spoke in the official tongue of the upwardly mobile — articulate, guardedly precise, and devoid of any personal flair — but with his own brother he felt obliged to revert to the patois of Lafitte Street and childhood. It was as if he was not certain that Shade could understand anything else.

"Righteous," Shade said. "Everything's wired, and that's on the maximum square, blood."

Francois had a longer face than his brother, with sharper, more Gallic features, and his eyes were hazel rather than blue, but there was equal belligerence in the lines of their jaws. He cocked one thick eyebrow at his brother's response.

"Been going to night school, eh, Rene?"

"Don't do that," Shade snapped. He had not finished college, had in fact only acted as if he intended to for one year, and Francois often intimated that this lack of letter-grade accreditation was a huge gulf between them. This regularly pissed Shade off, and he found that, for some reason, with a mysterious link to logic, blood relatives could spark his temper more surely and fiercely than any other members of the planet. "This is business, I thought. We can dozen it out some other time."

Francois hoisted his chin in silent agreement.

"Okay," he said. "Now, as I have it, Rankin surprised an intruder and was killed by the undoubtedly terrified individual. Perhaps because Rankin could identify him."

"Jesus shit," Shade said. He found himself walking to the same window the captain had been drawn to. "You're supposed to ride herd on me. They put my little fuckin' brother on me to make sure I only uncover the *right* dirt. I saw it comin', soon as I opened that door."

"Come on," Francois barked. "Look, I'm just here to coordinate things. You know, a lot of people are nervous about this case. Some nasty misunderstandings could come out of this if it's played to the crowd, man. You know that. So we need to straighten it out quickly." He then pushed up from the desk and faced his shorter brother. "Besides, I'm only a year younger."

"You haven't really been younger for a long time."

A smile spread Francois's thick lips.

"I know," he said.

A sort of fond sadness meandered through Shade. It was partly because he loved his brother and knew him perfectly, partly because he did not know him at all. The unlighted chamber where one's true and most secret longings and convictions are housed has a door that is impressively sealed. The more you turn the knob and peek through the keyhole, the more you have to guess, and the less you know.

"You sound proud to be older than you should be," Shade said.

"Oh," Francois breathed theatrically, "being young is an overrated sidetrack." He shrugged his shoulders like a wink. "I'm more impressed by the mainline of things."

"You're willing enough to pay the price of riding it."

"You pay the price, big bro, whether you ride *it* or *it* rides you. Let's be our ages, huh?"

There had been a time, not too long ago, when Francois had been energetic in his defense of the stepped-on multitudes, passionate in his pleas for those mendicants before the bar, those old neighborhood losers whose humanity he would not deny. He'd had a threat in his stance toward the system that had not always been kind to those close to him, and a mind quick to become belligerent in his quest of justice for the smallfry. Justice. But over the last few years something had changed, an unexpected metamorphosis brought on by the

89

passing of days. Marriage to a Hawthorne Hills lady; turning thirty; a series of educational connivings with triple-last-named deal cutters who groveled profitably, and only into golden cups; and consequent greenbacks. He still sought justice, but more and more, justice had become a pseudonym, an alias, for Francois Shade, late of Lafitte Street, but lately of Wyndham Lane.

"Okay," Shade said. "Lets us *do* talk some turkey. What's in this for you, ol' brother o' mine?"

Their eyes met and there was no shame or fear in either face.

"It's my job. For now." Francois made an excusing gesture with his hands. "This thing could have interesting ripples for years. Alvin Rankin was black, you know."

"I think I made a mental note of that, yes."

"Well, he was a good man. A good Democrat. It wouldn't be the worst thing for me to be the man who prosecuted on this. But that depends on whom I'm prosecuting, too."

"Ah. So if you can cook it up in a way that the party's skirts are entirely clean you might make city councilman, or something."

"Well, yes. But that's just the crudest bit of it. As far as cities are concerned, Rene, if you want to be elected in the next thirty years, you better have good rapport with blacks and Latins. A lot of whites aren't ready to understand that, but they're going to the hard way if they don't get with it."

"And this helps you there."

"It could. It's not a career maker, but, yes, it could help. I mean, any white pol who wants to be mayor and stay mayor had best take wide steps away from those old amusing Irish sorts of ways. It's quaint, but it won't play much longer."

"Well, thanks," Shade said. "That's fairly blunt."

Both men smiled, and Shade felt tickled by the vibrations of some strange, submerged pride, for he'd just been tipped by a knowing tout who had the extra grace of kinship. There was a kind of backroom pleasure in it, and he could see how a man could be captivated by the process of success.

"That's as blunt as it's going to get, too," Francois said. "And all this has put me in mind of our rather motley family constellation. To wit: how's Tip?"

"Nasty as always."

"That's reassuring. People keep mentioning him to me, you know. I wish he'd change his name."

Shade laughed.

"I have an idée fixe that *he* feels ditto about us."

"Hunh, I guess it can't be helped."

"Not much."

The brothers then got down, down to business. Shade soon found himself adrift, floating on a mirage of family interests, brotherly love, and sheer admiration of drive. He ended up agreeing to follow the burglary hope for one full day, so long as nothing solid developed along other avenues.

When they parted Francois said, "Think of the long run."

"I try to," Shade said. "I really do. But I can't quite feature it."

10

Lester Moeller, an unambitious ham-and-egger of a thief, with an eye for the backdoor possibilities but with such a spineless style of loose-change larceny that he seemed able only to lift enough to break even, shook his shaggy-haired head and raised his arms in a gesture of innocence.

"Really," he said in his sissy tone, looking first at Shade, then How Blanchette, "I mean, I ain't hardly been out of the house, let alone Pan Fry."

"Of course. Why would anyone want to leave this here castle?" asked Blanchette, his sweeping hand wave drawing attention to the hamburger wrappers on the floor, the shaky table nailed to the wall, and the windows that were gray-taped into their frames.

"All right," Lester said with an agreeing bob of his head. "I gotta leave to pee, sure. I'm not the sort who'll use the sink. And to pooh. The john here, it don't flush."

"Maybe you should get you one that does," Shade suggested. "Next time you go out, I mean."

Lester shook his head. He was young but he had come to know himself.

"I wouldn't have the exper-tise," he said. "That ain't shop-liftin', you know. You gotta know how to go about it. I can unplug electric sockets, but I don't know shit about plumbing."

"That's a shame," Shade said.

"Anyway, how would you stiff-leg a toilet down the street? A fella has to think about things like that, you know."

Years earlier, when Shade had still been slinging leather for a living, he'd come out of Brouilliard's Gym into the dirt alley parking lot in back and caught young Lester trying to liberate the contents of the glove compartment of his Nova. Shade, having never found much pleasure in battering obvious inferiors, refrained from striking Lester. He put an elbow around the bird-bone neck of the eighteen-year-old, then used his free hand to unbuckle his trousers. Then he shoved him down and pantsed him. As the fledgling thief scrambled in the sunlight for the cover of a nearby fire hydrant, Shade said, "I'll leave them in the mystery section of the library for you." When he drove away, Lester was kneeling behind the hydrant in a fitting pose.

"You have some serious defects as a thief, Lester."

"Well," Lester replied with a shrug of his thin, soft shoulders, "I'm not *too* good at anything."

Blanchette laughed.

"Your rap sheet'll back you up on that."

"At least I try," Lester said sullenly. "I could be on welfare, prob'ly."

Shade stood and unbuttoned another button of his shirt. His clothes felt like fresh paint, and sweat was beading on his forehead. He looked at Blanchette, who was amazingly still in his slenderizing trench coat. Was vanity more powerful than heat? he wondered.

"Well, shit, Lester," Shade said. "You're not tellin' me anything I want to hear. What's the point of us bein' friends if you can't tell me what I want to hear?"

"Come on, don't tease me," Lester said. "You don't like me. We never was friends." He raised his round brown eyes and looked Shade square in the face. "Nobody likes me and I always been knowin' that, so cut the mean shit."

"If you hear anything, though."

"Right. But nobody I know does much over in Pan Fry, man. They catch us over there, man, they got some stick-and-ball games they play with you. Guess who's the ball?"

"I'm convinced," Shade said. "You sold me. But don't let me find out you're lyin'."

It was Lester's turn to laugh.

"I guess you'd bust me then, huh? Send me to some terrible place."

Shade and Blanchette joined in on the chuckle as well, for Lester was of the self-mutated breed that was at least as happy locked up as free. Slamming steel doors were home cooking, mama's milk and cookies, to him.

"Uh-uh, you'd like that too much," Shade said. "Next time we pop you we're goin' to pass the hat, take up a collection, and send you to vocational-technical so you can learn just enough about power tools to kill your fool self."

"I've lived through worse," Lester said as he followed the detectives to the door.

Once outside on the lean, hard-bricked street, Shade and Blanchette paused to decide what pointless visit to make next.

"It's almost four," Blanchette said. "We're losin' the day. None of these twerps is goin' to break into a councilman's house, then get confused about what they're there for, and decide to whack a guy for free, you know. Since they're already there."

"You know that and I know that, but nobody else gives a fuck."

Blanchette held his trench coat open and fanned himself with the flaps. In the following silence he walked to a parked car and sat on the hood. His short legs dangled over the fender and he scrutinized the goo-coated sidewalk as if it were a mirror. He humphed from time to time and sweat ran down his face like cracks in a porcelain Buddha.

"I just don't like it," Shade said. "If we don't do what we know we should someone else is goin' to get it."

"It won't be our fault."

"Nothing's our fault."

"Should have that on our badges, you ask me."

"Everything's our fault."

"Oh, boy. Don't start with that schoolboy bullshit again, Rene. Today ain't the day for it."

The sun rebounded off nearby windows, and heat rose from the concrete walk, giving agony extra angles to work.

"Sundown Phillips," Shade said.

Blanchette pursed his lips, then began to nod.

"That's true," he said. "If anybody knows what's happenin' in Pan Fry, he's it."

"Yeah. What say let's be sociable and go visiting, huh?"

"Okay, partner," Blanchette said in a strangely soft tone. "I was wonderin' how long we were goin' to humor that cashmere brother of yours. I was goin' to lose faith if it was more than another ten minutes, to tell you the truth."

Nodding, Shade said, "You and me both."

In the aspiring self-mythology of Saint Bruno, a town that liked to refer to itself as a baby Chicago, there were grapevine

95

Roykos and street-corner Sandburgs who found odd connections between the Windy City on the Lake and the Wheezing Town on the River.

The pecking order of the homegrown juice merchants and trigger jerkers, green-felt Caesars, and snow-shoveling cowboys was likened to a vivid Chicago of the memory. And in this urban simile, if Auguste Beaurain, a force so devious, potent, and dangerous that he'd never even been hooked for a parking ticket, was a scaled-down Capone, and Steve Roque an irritating Spike O'Donnell, then surely Sundown Phillips of Pan Fry was perfectly Bugs Moran.

The detectives pulled into the graveled space in front of the wood-frame house that served as an office for Phillips Construction. There were two green pickup trucks and a motorcycle parked outside. A large dog with long strands of mud for hair, and a disturbingly narrow head, relaxed on the porch.

The dog rose as the detectives approached and Shade dropped a hand to scratch around where the ears should be. The dog sighed, then lay back down and Shade opened the door.

There was a small front room with a somber gang of gray filing cabinets spread around against the walls, and a receptionist's desk that was unattended.

The detectives stepped into the middle of the room and stopped. There was a picture of Martin Luther King on one wall, high up and centered, with signed photos of Satchel Paige, Itzhak Perlman, and Tina Turner on display beneath.

Shade stepped over to a white door in the corner of the room and knocked.

After a long pause the door drawled open to reveal a table circled by curious faces. A thin, butterscotch man with a Vandyke beard and a taste for clothes that were tropical in theme blocked Shade's entrance.

"This is business hours," the man said. "You got business?"

At the table in the background one of the curious faces suddenly became less so, and shoved away from the table, then stood. From topknot to toe there was a length of body that could've maintained a decent rushing average by consistently collapsing forward. Sundown Phillips was a grade or two above large, with a leonine process of hair, and dark skin.

As he approached the door he began to smile.

"Well, well, if it's not Tomatuh Can Shade," he said with a roll of his eyes. "The Con-tend-uh!"

Shade made the Vandyke beard as Powers Jones, an occasional carpenter and full-time suspect, who worked for Phillips. He couldn't see the other faces well enough to identify them.

Sundown filled the doorway and blocked his view. His smile was as friendly as a holding cell. He backed Shade up, stepped into the main room, and pulled the white door closed.

"What's this?" Blanchette asked, leaning forward conspiratorially. "A little early in the day for a Tupperware party, ain't it?"

Sundown responded by looking down on Blanchette with an amused curl to his lips.

"See the sign outside?" Sundown asked. "This *is* a business."

"Look, Phillips," Shade said. "I want to ask you a few things."

"About what?"

"About yourself."

"Why, how nice," Sundown said. "Six-seven, two seventy, black nappy over brown, a long jagged liverish-looking one under the left armpit, and, well, like a donkey. I believe that covers the vitals."

Blanchette, who stood nose to nipple on Sundown, said, "Most people don't like wiseasses."

"Is that so? I'd like to see the dem-o-graphic breakdown on that poll."

There were certain situations in which Blanchette was of little use. Shade quickly assessed this to be one of them and asked How to wait in the car. Blanchette, however, was in need of his self-image as a ruggedly chubby, knockaround cop who had yet to encounter humanity in dimensions that could back him down.

"Okay," he said. "All right. But if it don't work your way, Shade, then it'll be time for mine."

As the door clinked shut behind Blanchette, Sundown sat on the receptionist's desk. He opened a button on his yellow summer cotton shirt, and buffed his boot tips on the back of his slacks.

"What is it, Shade?"

"That meeting in there," Shade flicked his head toward the white door, "it's about Rankin, right? You guys already carvin' up the leftovers or what?"

"Man, you got a lot of nerve, you know that? Why the fuck shouldn't we be talkin' about Alvin? We all knew him, you see. He was our man, and on the upswing, too. You think of anything more important that's gone down lately?"

"I was wonderin' if you might know who remodeled his head, or anything like that."

Sundown held his arms out, then quickly glanced down the length of both limbs.

"I don't see any feathers," he said. "And my voice ain't turned into no coo-coo sort of thing." He dropped his enormous arms back to his sides. "So what makes you think I got any statements to make?"

"I don't know. Some people feel grief, you know, Phillips, when someone they care about gets whacked."

"Grief? Grief gets action in my world, honey, not any of them fuckin' useless tears and God-hollers and such shit."

The white door opened and Powers Jones stuck his head out.

"Are we waitin' or what?" he asked.

"Or what," Sundown said. He paced about the room, then checked his watch. "It's Rochelle time, anyhow." He pointed at Jones. "Just sit tight." His long legs two-stepped to the door. "You want to talk to me, Shade, then you follow along. Otherwise, au revoir, tadpole."

They went outside and Shade gestured to Blanchette to stay put. The two men did not speak as they traveled down the sidewalk, a sidewalk that disappeared at times, and then reappeared, roller-coasted by the roots of timeless trees that would not be diverted by mere concrete.

"I got to pick up my daughter," Sundown said. "I don't like her walkin' around alone out here. You know. She takes piano after school. She's goin' to be a Keith Jarrett someday, only prettier."

"Hey, hey, hey."

This was the same man, Shade reflected, who'd played high school football like a Greek god with a score to settle, a personal vendetta that encompassed all who would dare suit up against him. He was famous for his grudge clobberings of opponents he decided he liked least, whether they carried the ball or stood on the sidelines. His style kept many an anemic offensive drive alive with penalties, but he also stopped plenty with bone-fracturing hits. He'd had the speed of a tailback, despite his size, but the dementia of his play caused even Wishbone coaches to shy away from him. The word on the street was that he ran his new enterprises of loan-sharking, gambling, and miscellaneous larceny with the same brutal logic.

Despite an odd respect for the talented evilness of the man, Shade wanted to be the guy who dropped the flag on him for a long penalty.

Several young boys in rags wheeled spider bikes from out of alleys and began to flit around the men. The boys popped wheelies that landed very near the men, then exercised their audacity by requesting quarters to stop. "I could scuff your shoes for nothin'," they said, "but when a quarter's in my hand I miss them clean." When it became clear that no protection money would be forthcoming the pint-sized entrepreneurs drifted back into the familiar alleys they'd come out of.

"Trash," Sundown said. "They can't help it. They'll never know Bartók from Bootsy's Rubber Band."

"Right," Shade said with a nod. "There's plenty to be sad about in this life."

The school was of Depression-era vintage, with the high craftsmanship and charming fine points that grateful artisans had willingly, and cheaply, rendered. The bricks were darkened by generations of soot and smoke, but the character of the James Audubon School was still formidable.

"Maybe you could peddle some dope to the kids while we're here," Shade said.

"Hah," Sundown snorted. "You're out of touch, honey. It's the teachers who want dope now. They need it more."

"I see. So you're an asset to public education?"

"I *do* have that civic sense, yes."

The basketball courts and baseball diamond behind the school were surrounded by a high fence and gates that were heavily padlocked after hours, but democracy had asserted itself and several low passageways had been slashed through the chain links. At this hour the gates were just being locked, and a small, pretty berry of a girl in a yellow dress with red knee socks and a sheaf of sheet music in her hands stood waiting on the sidewalk.

This was turning out to be as much a waste as Lester, Shade thought. So Phillips's people were stunned, but not beyond alertness for gain. Who was?

"Rochelle," Sundown called.

The young girl started toward him. A true smile crossed her face and she started to skip to her father, but then she reclaimed her dignity and slid back into a more stately stride.

Sundown leaned to her face and kissed her cheek.

This, Shade thought, is the same man who the most secret of secret whispers said had knotted two St. Louis Syrians together by their arms, then sent them bobbing for rocks in a remote slough.

"We listened to Chopin today, Dad," Rochelle said brightly. "But we practiced 'Yankee Doodle Dandy.'"

"Look," Shade said. "This is heartwarming and all, but I need to know a few things."

"Correction. A lot of things."

"That's trite. No score. Now we can talk here like citizens, or on Second Street like what we are. Suit yourself."

"Come on," Sundown said. "I don't know what it's all about. If I did you think I'd be sittin' around my office *talkin'*?"

"Is that all you're doin'?"

A car horn began to honk, and Shade turned to see Blanchette squealing up the street in the city-issue Chevy. When the car was abreast of Shade it stopped, and Blanchette called out, "Come on! There's something on Seventh Street, and it's ours."

Without a word Shade jumped into the car, grateful for action, eager for a problem he could wrap his hands around.

101

11

Eventually he recognized the river. He'd been running near it for many minutes before he realized that the great, flat, flowing noodle of murk was a signpost back to the apartment. But was he going the right way?

Jewel tried to judge directions. Was that east? Or south? No handy mossed trees to clear things up, so it's all a toss-up. His face was scarlet in the cheeks, with webs of sweat running down his body. The blond pompadour that he usually doted on had now warped into fashions of desperate design.

No, that's the sun. It is. That's the sun!

Ooh, that man's head was bad frayed but maybe he never did die.

But this way, this way is home. That's the sun!

Although his lungs were clawing at his heart, he began to run once more. He followed the railroad tracks that paralleled the river. The woods were thick between the tracks and the water, but there were cracked-glass warehouses full of lunch-bucket men, and coal bins with roofs and lattice-planked walls on the other side. Too many people here. Some of them turned their faces on him. They looked strange.

Wads of paper were punched by the breeze and rattled like screams along the tracks. Occasionally suspicious heads popped up on the brush side and studied him before disappearing once more. Everywhere was now really a passing strange place.

They hate me. They talk. They hate me and they talk.

And I did do it.

His feet sank in the gravel between ties, sounding like a sprout of chains that he was going to have to get used to dragging.

When the heartscratch of exhaustion was becoming too much, he rounded a bend. He saw the tarnished copper dome of a church with a cross aged black atop it.

That's it.

Frayed head and shells talk hate me all over.

That's it! That's home up there!

Pete Ledoux stepped carefully down the slabwood stairs to the basement, dipping his head at the overhang. Even the clearest of plans can be warped by events into a bog of confusion, he'd found out this day, and now he wanted to pass the buck to Steve Roque.

Mrs. Roque, a knowing and pleasingly plump woman in jeans and jewelry, had shown him to the basement door. In the musty basement with green-painted cement walls, he located his boss in gym shorts and T-shirt, exercising to keep some order behind the treacherous expansion of his gut. He explained the new situation as Roque did sit-ups.

At the completion of one hundred sit-ups, Roque stood.

Ledoux had ended his canted recitation of the day and sat on an old chair, silently waiting.

Roque raked his fingers through his moist gray hair, then picked up dumbbells and began to do curls.

"What a fuckup," he said between clenched teeth, at about the fifteenth curl.

"You're awful strong, Steve," Ledoux said, when he realized those were eighty-pound weights.

"Rheumatic fever," Roque said. "I lost most of my hair at sixteen. And ever since I turned bald, I got serious about muscles."

"Well, I don't know — you look sort of good bald."

"That's 'cause you've never seen me with hair." Roque laid the dumbbells down. "*I've* never seen me with hair, either, really. Not as a man."

"Some women like bald guys," Ledoux said, nodding at his own perceptions. "Even if they wasn't barkers themselves, and could have a guy with hair, why they'd rather take a bald one. I've seen it happen."

"Listen, fuckup," Roque said crisply. "Don't pull that soft-con shit with me, hear?" Roque toweled sweat from his face and neck. "I mean, that's a real boost to my confidence and all, Pete, but I was wonderin' how much pussy you figure me to cop up in the joint?"

Roque tossed the towel to the floor and stared at Ledoux, who looked away.

"Maybe, though," Roque went on, "you think I could be real happy over at the pen, now, in Jeff City, since I got lucky and went bald during high school, but bald is in now? I won't have to be the lonely guy on the cell block, this time. Lots of ivory-assed canteen turnouts'll be wantin' to oil down my special bald head, you figure?"

104

Ledoux studied his feet with an embarrassed slump to his body.

"Now, you're startin' to talk negative, Steve. Nobody has us on this, mon ami."

"The kid has you. You have me. Is that nothin'?" Roque stood spread-legged and tapped his belly. "It's like one coil of the noose leads to another."

"Well, you're right. The kid's a problem."

"The kid's a problem to you, fuckup." Roque stripped his soggy shirt off and hurled it toward the washer and dryer in the far corner. "You're a problem to me."

With his chin cupped in one hand and the other fanning the clammy air, Ledoux said, "I don't see where *I'm* a problem. To nobody."

"As long as the kid's a problem—you're a problem."

"That kid's goin' to die."

"Sure he is," Roque said. "But you stay away from him. You already fucked it up pretty good and now we can't go near him. He's too hot for us."

"Maybe I could have his cousin whack him. Diddle his girl once or twice, then whack him in the head." Ledoux hopefully wagged his eyebrows, and inclined his head toward Roque. "Now you might peddle that as your basic crime of passion, if the cousin's dick's still wet, you know. It could work."

"No. You're very clever at dumb shit, fuckup, but I think I'll nix that plot."

Roque stood under the lone light bulb and did side-to-side cool-down stretches. There were purple gouges in the small of his back, and several thin crisscross scars on his chest.

"Where'd you get those bites taken out of your back?"

"Frozen Chosen. That was Korea. Mortar shower."

"Ah. That's kind of neat, really. They didn't take me."

"Bad heart or something?"

"Nah. I'm a crook from the cradle. They don't want crooks who admit it. You should've told them."

"Yeah. But actually I wasn't much of a crook yet, at the time."

"The war grew you up, eh, mon ami?"

"Something did."

"You got to follow your talent," Ledoux said. "That's no sin." He gestured at Roque's hairy chest. "Those slits on your titties, there — those from the same mortar?"

"Uh-uh. That's razor blades, from the neighborhood. I had a point, but I should've kept quiet about it."

When he'd finished his stretches Roque sat down on the weight bench. His expression was smooth, nicely calmed by the workout, late-coming sweat dripping from his nose.

"I'm going to tell you what to do, dipshit. Then you'll do it."

"You know I will. If it can be done."

"I never mistook you for Superman, take my word. This is something you can handle. We can't go to the kid, now, and peg him in the neighborhood. Everybody knows us down there. So what you're going to do is, you're going to call Sundown Phillips and you're going to tip our peckerwood shooter in to them. Say it's because you don't want no misunderstandings, just because the kid's workin' out of Frogtown."

"But why would I do that?"

"You dumb-ass. You don't even make me laugh, you know that? Use your fuckin' noodle, will you? You say something like you've been told this kid did it, robbery or something, and you're giving him up for peace, that's all."

"They'll go in and kill him."

"No shit? Have I told you how dumb I think you are lately? I mean, no shit, Pete—if we're lucky they'll kill him."

Ledoux stood, his legs not quite steady, and nodded toward his boss.

"You're the man," he said. "I'll go do it. But I got to say I don't like tellin' niggers they can come into Frogtown, you know, and shoot a white man."

"Grow up, Pete. Get the niggers out of your nightmares and grow up. It's business."

"I hear you talkin', but I don't like it, lettin' 'em come in down here on their own and kill a white man. It could start a trend. I don't like it. But I'll do it 'cause you say to do it." He faced away from Roque. "Nothin' else could make me."

Roque lay back on the workout bench and shaded his eyes with his hands.

"So long, Pete," he said. "It's time to cut fresh bait and fish deep. Don't fall in."

The inside of his car was still baking hot, and everything liquid in him seemed to be dripping down his neck. Ledoux drove along the cobblestone street where cars were jammed to the curb, and kids played fuzzball between passing vehicles. This was it: aged brick row houses; idly athletic punks; twelve-year-old cars; and ancient litter. Home. Ledoux had protected this ground many times in his life, stretching all the way back to when he was ten, and the south-side Germans had come in three quick cars to seek revenge for some slight to their vanity that was now long forgotten. He'd broken his wrist that day when knocked on top of it by a grim-faced Dutch Boy who was at least fifteen, twice his size, and no fan of fair play. There had been many such days, and nights, run consecutively to make a life.

And now he was inviting Pan Fry to forget old scores and

come on down and waste a white man. Or two, or three. Aw, things change so much.

But better it be him than me. That never changed.

Someday he would have it worked out so no man could treat him like Roque did. That was a life plan. But business came first.

At a pay phone outside Langlois's Package Liquor Store, he pulled over. The hinges creaked as he shoved his way into the booth. The walls were mightily embellished with liquored taunts and slurs and several sloppily scrawled but robustly recommended phone numbers. He thought about how he had spoken to Teejay Crane a week or ten days earlier.

"Look," Ledoux had said as they huddled in the lobby of Crane's theater, "Roque has got you. I don't know your excuse for why he's got you, man, but he's got you by the nads."

Teejay Crane's nose was tapered at the bridge and bellbottomed at the base. "A brother man sold me out," he said. "That's all that gives Steve a complaint with me."

"I don't think that's it," Ledoux said. "I think it's that you owe him money you ain't paid. Steve's one of these sensitive guys, you know. He don't like gettin' fucked over."

"Who does?"

"You, I guess," Ledoux said. "You go into hock to rev up a little coke and a live pussy show here, in this joint, only Sundown whatchamajigaboo don't like you free-lancing. He's down on your independence. In fact, that's why you're gettin' shylocked by Roque. But then you get popped by the cops who seem to know exactly what you're up to and in what room. And now you tell me you ain't sure you want to square things up." Ledoux wagged a finger in Crane's face. "That to me sounds like a guy who sort of *likes* gettin' fucked over."

Crane leaned against the stair banister to rest his lame right leg. There were salty patches in his black hair and he didn't look as though he'd slept too well lately.

"I needed the green to grease things," he said. "Sundown, he's one stingy nigger. He wouldn't allow me to start out on my own. Like, you know, my little bit of action might keep one or two pennies from rollin' into his own big pocket. So I had to grease things on my own, all the way up to Alvin Rankin."

"You think."

"I know. I know 'cause Alvin called me and gave me about two breaths of warning that I was gettin' raided. Said he couldn't help me. Said he had bigger fish to fry." Crane sighed and shook his head. "To my mind that man is just another snake. Give him your votes and he forgets where he got them. He could've stood up for me, but Sundown leaned on him to let me go down. I know that's how it was."

"Yeah," Ledoux said, "it's like, I sympathize with you, Crane. You're givin' my heart a nosebleed, no question about it. But if you want *me* off your case you got to get straight with us. Especially Steve. He'd rather waste a welsher than eat apple pie, if you know what I mean."

"I understand that," Crane said. "But try to see it from my side."

"What I see from your side is a guy who's in trouble and won't try to get out of it. Rankin robbed you, you asshole."

Crane reared up his head at this.

"Yeah," Ledoux said, "asshole. I said it. You're an asshole. The man robbed you to keep you a peon and you'd still rather die than get even with him. I mean, you know you're goin' to die, don't you? If you don't get Rankin for us."

"I've had that suspicion."

"It's a fact."

Crane stood erect and walked to the door. "I'll talk to Steve," he said. "I know I'm in a spot."

"Your whole fuckin' family is."

But Crane was out of the spot now, Ledoux thought grimly as he dumped the coins into the telephone slot and dialed the number, feeling worse than he had all day.

On the third ring the phone was answered.

"Phillips Construction. Powers Jones talkin'."

"I want to talk to Phillips."

"Ain't here. Who is this?"

"Nobody."

"This Pete Ledoux, ain't it?"

"So?"

"You got somethin' to say, say it."

There was a long pause, a pause long enough for several decades to be overruled.

"Yeah. I got somethin' to say. You be sure and tell it to Phillips. What it is, is this . . ."

12

The crowd was pressing forward, butting against the police cordon of three black-and-whites, their expressions a fusion of the horrified and the entertained. They gawked loose-jawed at the body of Teejay Crane, unified in their fondness for the misery of strangers.

At 5:46 Detectives Shade and Blanchette arrived on the scene. They approached a knot of officers in uniform and shirt-sleeved detectives who stood around the body. A departing patrolman grabbed Shade by the arm.

"Jesus, it's a mess," the young patrolman said.

"Never seen brains before?" Blanchette asked.

"Not in so many different places."

Detective Tom Gutermuth, a liver-spotted, mellow, robbery detail man, who'd happened on the scene first, told Shade that there was not, in fact, much to tell. Blond kid with Elvis ambitions, waving a sawed-off, point-blank, two shots.

The weapon has been found and black-and-whites are cruising for the shooter. The victim was the owner-operator of the Olde Sussex Theater, and there were witnesses.

"A porno prince," Blanchette said.

"Right," Shade said. "We should pull in everybody we see in stained raincoats, I reckon."

"And shitpaper stuck to their shoes."

There seemed to be no benefit in standing around scrutinizing the corpse, so Shade decided to do what he thought he was best at: trail a danger through the hard streets and volatile alleys of Saint Bruno. Something, at least, might be turned up through action that contemplation would let slip away.

Blanchette stayed at the scene, and Shade set off alone, on foot.

The blond shooter had definitely made an impression. His passing had been memorable and Shade had no difficulty following his route from the Olde Sussex to Second Street. Shade would tap on windows and ask loiterers if they'd seen a panicked whitebread with lunacy in his eyes. Although the area was a mix in terms of race, the ambiance was black. The thumping bass backbeats that echoed from nearby sound systems were of sepia artistry, and the voices, even those of the honkoid denizens, rapped black. They always remembered the blond but rarely spoke, only pointed "that way," toward the river.

Shade began to trot down the streets, knowing that he was most of an hour behind. The retail businesses had closed as a rule, and only taverns, the Woolworth's, and video arcades were open. He paused to ask questions in the arcades, thus giving every would-be wiseass and nascent tough guy the chance to define himself by his response. Adolescent drollery and derivative insolence. Shade didn't have the time for it, so he turned toward the river and began to lope.

He was winding back toward the edge of Frogtown. The blond seemed to have been set on a course to the river and once there he could only go south, or north to Frogtown. Instinct and long experience prompted Shade to follow the northern chance.

Rousseau Street flanked the river. It was a street of warehouses, flophouses, and Jesus missions, peopled by winos, the perpetually hard of luck, and one or two who were roughly saints. Coal bins lined the tracks, providing a haven for those rambling men who couldn't spare the buck for a flop and refused to perjure themselves on the God issue for the payoff bowl of soup and green-blanketed bunk. Urban Darwinism was at work in the grim light of this place, and the mean got over with their no-limit rage, while the weak went under, silently.

Shade approached a quartet of men who were joined in a medley of petty frustrations and narcissistic defeats. Two of the men were gray, with features matted by time, and the others were working toward the same transformation.

"A blond came by here," Shade said. "He was running, probably. See him?"

"I ain't seen nobody I *wanted* to see since Glenn Miller died," one of the grayed men said.

"Blond, huh?" said one of the less grayed men. "Blond. My friend Terry is blond. Sort of dishwater blond. I like him, he likes me. But he lives in Memphis, you know. That's not here."

"Right," Shade said. He turned to the youngest-looking member of the group. "You see the kid I'm talkin' about?"

The man shook his head.

"I never do," he said. "That's a credo, you."

"I knew it was," Shade said, and loped on.

Further along the worn-down street, Shade, remembering

113

the mornings of his youth when a sport involving rocks and taunts had been made of the passed-out losers who slept in the woods near the river, thought about searching those woods. He stopped in front of the Holy Order of Man, a Catholic snooze joint, and decided that it would take too many searchers to do it right.

He heard something knocking and turned to see a man with purple thumbprints beneath his eyes motioning to him from the doorway of the Holy Order.

"You're the law," the man said, raspily. His skin had the pallor of sickness, or asceticism, and his head had been recently shaved. "You're standin' around with your thumb up your ass, and I'm sayin' to myself, 'That man is with the law.'" The man scraped a kitchen match along the windowsill and lit a smoke. "Am I right?"

"How'd you know?" Shade asked, although an ability to spot cops was not, in his experience, a particularly rare skill.

"I'm a lay brother," the man said, displaying his yellow teeth. "But there was a time I'd get in your upstairs window and get out again with your RCA TV and your stash of Trojans while you're takin' a two-beer leak. Then one time some citizen didn't nail his gutter in exactly solid and I fell." He blew smoke and nodded. "I was caught, but I woke up knowin' Our Lord real well."

"Mysterious ways."

"Cheap nails."

"I'm lookin' for somebody."

"No joke?"

"Blond kid, on the run."

"Did he do bad things?"

"Yes," Shade said. "He did bad."

"Well, I'm sure Our Lord still loves him."

"Our Lord should've stopped him."

114

The man inhaled like a whistle, then shrugged and exhaled a serpent of smoke.

"The Lord's not that possessive," he said. "That's a good thing about the love of Our Lord, you know. He's not at all what you'd call *clingy,* but keeps pretty cool about the whole affair."

"Uh-huh," Shade grunted. "I've noticed that."

"But I'm a new man these days. I'll even tell *you* something. I saw the sinner ye seek."

"Which way did he go?"

The man pointed north along the tracks.

"Yonder. He'd seen the Devil. It was in his eyes and he was stumblin'." The man looked Shade in the eye and nodded. "I never much helped the law before, and you know what? It don't make me feel any better, copper."

"Keep doin' it till you get off parole, though, won't you?"

Shade set off at a fast pace. It was only a few more blocks to Frogtown and he covered that ground quickly. A few times he passed people who sensed his quarry, stopped, and pointed north, north to the neighborhood he'd spent his whole life in. A splotch of houses and memories, failures and rancid conquests, a small scoop of earth that he knew more deeply than he knew his own father.

It had certainly given him more guidance.

13

Powers Jones, the butterscotch shooter whose clothes had a floral, South Seas theme, moved down Voltaire Street like a stealthy hurricane. He paused at the Chalk & Stroke. The door was propped open in the hopes of attracting a breeze, but drew only flies. Powers stood in the doorway and scanned the crowd. It was the sort of poolroom that required air you could shake hands with before you breathed it, and husky smoke made it so. There was nothing there to interest him, so Powers Jones walked on.

A Ford station wagon was keeping pace with the tropical stranger, but stayed several yards behind him. He motioned to it from time to time, and shook his head. Finally Powers halted across the street from a crotchety hair salon and looked above it to a ramshackle window where a lamp shone in the dusk. He signaled to the Ford to park down the block a few car lengths, then walked to it.

He opened the rear door and ducked into the seat. There were two young black men in the front. Powers rested his elbows on the seat back and scooted forward.

"This the place," he said. "Farm boy's crib. Time to earn your beans."

The driver checked the street with a stiff-necked swivel, so cool he was almost paralyzed. The other accomplice, clearly a freshman on the mayhem squad, was openly nervous.

"I just watch the door," he said. "I've did that before."

Powers Jones lit a Salem and leaned back in the seat.

"I'll be doin' what has to be," he said. "So hang loose, Thomas. We can't move till we sure the cracker there, anyhow."

"The light's on," Thomas said.

"Yeah, well, it could be to keep thieves back, you know. We wait till we certain he's in there."

"When will that be?"

"Huh, huh," Powers chuckled. "It'll be when that fool cracker start hangin' his nose out the window. And he will, if he there, 'cause he real jittery, and he got to be devastatin' dumb. Huh, huh." Powers Jones propped his feet on the front seat so that they dangled between the two trainees. "He so silly *everybody* want him dead."

Suze leaned against the bathroom door and knocked again. She was wearing her blue two-piece swimsuit with the white polka dots that were juggled when she walked. She bent down to the doorknob as if it were an intercom.

"Come on, baby," she said. "Come out of there. It's your special favorite — fish sticks and fried okra." There was no response. "Are you sick? You looked sick. Don't eat in these cafes around here. I see 'em feedin' cats at night, but their

117

faces don't really look that kind. Eat what comes in a bag. That's sanitary."

He'd come in half an hour earlier with hair twisted into a nest, his face blood-red wherever it wasn't deathly pale, and his clothes all wet. The first thing he'd done was get his pistol from the dresser. Suze asked him what was up. He'd smiled then in a way that made her chest feel bubbly. "Oh, just gonna see somethin', is all." He'd been in the bathroom and silent ever since.

"Look, Jewel — should I throw it out, or what? It won't stay crisp, you know."

The lock scraped and the door opened. Jewel's hair was combed, and his face had been washed, but his eyes were twitching.

"Now there's my baby," Suze said, and threw her arms around his neck. She leaned into him lustily and rubbed her breasts to his chest. Her right leg slid into the inviting gap left by the spread of his, and she forced a bumping of groins. "Mmmm."

"I didn't eat no cat," he said stiffly. "That's awful."

"Good. That's good. I cooked you your special favorite." Suze began to slither encouragingly against his sensitive regions, then hung a finger in her mouth and tried to look smoldering. "Baby, you started me off this mornin' with a certain sort of ideas. I've had 'em all day long. That made your sweet magnolia get, you know, a little damp."

Jewel rested his hand on the pistol in his belt, then eased Suze away.

"I'm not sick."

A sweet giggle came from Suze.

"To be honest, I patted it dry with my fingers 'cause I didn't know *when* you'd get here." She pushed herself up close to

him and turned her face up to his. "Twice. And I was startin'
to look at the ketchup bottle funny, too." She laughed.

"I don't think I can eat," Jewel said. He turned away.
"There's things in this world that is really gonna shock
you, girl."

"Aw, Jewel," Suze whined and walked to the couch. "What
is it with you, anyhow?" She flopped onto the couch, knowing that her plans for the evening were off. "What's the
matter?"

"Men business."

"You meet you some gal who's got a car or somethin'?"

"I told you, girl, men business."

"Well now, that don't tell me just a whole hell of a lot, does
it? I mean, you been playin' baseball or shootin' rabbits, or
what?"

Jewel walked to the window and stuck his head between
the curtains. There was still light to the day and there were
plenty of people on the street, but none who meant anything
to him. He went back to the couch and sat on the thick
padded arm.

"Did you steal somethin', baby?"

"Don't ask."

"You've done that before and not got caught. Don't get
worried up about it. There's lots more thieves up here than
back home. They won't even think of you around here."

Jewel pulled the pistol from his belt and set it on the couch
beside him. He saw his guitar with the snapped E string still on
the floor where it had dropped after he flung it away that
morning. While staring at it he drifted into thought, one finger
motionless at the side of his nose.

"Jew-el, tell me what's goin' on."

He blinked several times.

119

"We're not married," he said finally. "They could make you tell on me."

"But I wouldn't. I never would do that."

"Oh, yeah," Jewel said, then stood. "Sure." He began to pace, then suddenly stopped. "Do you know somethin' you shouldn't? What do you know?"

An unexpected boom resounded from the apartment door, then another, and the door drunkenly wobbled open. And a bouquet of flowers with a man inside it stepped through pointing a long-stemmed pistol.

Jewel ran toward the rear of the apartment. There was a window in the back with smoked glass that he'd never been able to lift, and he didn't know what it opened onto, but finely tuned fear instantly propelled him toward it.

"Don't talk," Powers Jones announced, then took a wild shot at Jewel in the shadows.

Squealing, Suze rolled onto her back on the couch, covering the pistol, and curled into a baby-nap ball, her scant costume flexed taut.

Powers pointed the pistol at her.

"Oh, yes," he said, then followed Jewel.

Thomas stepped inside the door, a silver automatic in his hand. His feet kept moving as if he were stamping out a grass fire, and the pistol aimed at everything at least once.

The damn window naturally wouldn't open, as Jewel had suspected that it wouldn't, even with life on the line, and all he could find nearby was a frying pan with a layer of pork grease thickened in it. He picked it up by the wooden handle and began to beat at the window, pig essence and glass chips splattering up his arms and chest.

"He's got to have a gun!" Thomas yelled. "Watch it!"

Slowly, Powers Jones edged along the wall of the dim hallway, waiting for the split-second meeting that would end this thing and raise his asking price in the future.

The frying pan thumped and glass could be heard tinkling down.

The pistol was a dull ache in the small of Suze's back, then her hand found it and some basic instinct for combat took over. The flowery spade was most definitely the more dangerous, this took her but a blink to decide, and she rolled off the couch, knowing that life was a miracle, lobbing bullets toward the handiest danger.

The bullets whacked the walls of the hallway and grooved gashes in the ceiling, dropping a fine drywall mist.

"She's shootin'!" Thomas yelled now. "Get her!"

Powers Jones was suddenly flat on his heaving belly in the dark hallway of a redneck nigger-killer's hovel, with a lame for a partner and a white-trash mama trying to snuff him by sheer luck.

"Give me some help!" he hollered. "God damn, Thomas, she right by you!" There was no answer. "Thomas!"

The bathroom door had a lock on it, as every secret lipsticker knew, and locks kept people out. Suze made an acrobatic leap into the john, and slammed the door shut, then twisted the lock. She faced the door and sank in the corner between the tub and the toilet, her legs splayed out, the pistol on her lap.

Powers Jones raised himself to his knees and paused.

The window looked out over the rear room of the downstairs hair salon and an alley. There were jigsaw scales of glass still in the panes, but Jewel hurled himself through, then fell the six feet to the roof below. He was ripped on both sides but the cuts didn't hurt, not like the jolt of landing did.

Abandoning stealth and cool, Powers Jones sprinted to the

rear window and leaned out of it. He snapped two shots at Jewel, then watched as he rolled off the roof and out of sight. A woman with blue hair had been standing in the alley, patting her new do as she inspected herself in a compact mirror. Her mouth was now a grimace and she stared at the window.

"You get out of here!" she barked.

Powers met her gaze, then lazily shook his head.

"Forget you," he said.

He started toward the apartment entrance. Thomas had now come into the room and was waving his pistol at the bathroom door.

"In there," he said. "She's in there."

Adopting his most withering look, Powers Jones glared into the younger man's face, then stepped quickly past him and out the door.

"Hey, wait, man," Thomas said. "I watched the door, didn't I?"

He looked from john to exit, indecisive, then blasted three rounds into the john. The wood splintered, something thick shattered, and there was a sharp shriek, then a moan. Thomas backed out of the apartment lest the wounded fox come back tough, his pistol at the ready. At the door he turned and saw that he was being left behind, shuddered, then ran.

14

It must be voodoo, Jewel thought. Some brand of voodoo that's connected by the clouds, or city pigeons, maybe. Some nigger magic is at work, that's certain — how else could they find me so quick?

Jewel moved down the alley in an original gait that had the stealth of a chorus line and the speed of a paranoid diva. Run, drop to the ground, look for cover, stare toward the rooftops, then spring up and run some more.

His sides did not hurt, really, but sometimes there was a pesky stinging. He put his hands over the cuts, one on each love handle, and tried to stop the bleeding. But for something that didn't really hurt, those cuts bled a lot.

Night was beginning to lower a protective veil of darkness, but Jewel's passage was not secret. The sidewalk was skittering with people who'd had a lifetime of experience in looking the other way while still noticing the shoe style and wallet potential of those they'd never seen before, officer. Honest.

Jewel was aware of everyone. His hands at his sides had droplets of blood bulging on the fingertips, and he looked down to watch them plop to the concrete. The trajectory of his vein-dribbles bombing the sidewalk occasionally caused him to stop. He stood still with hopelessness as the weight of the droplets built, then gently swayed his body to aim the blood at cracks, cigar stubs, or shards of glass.

There was altogether too much strangeness afoot in this place. People went around you, heads turned the other way, but they knew you were running. Look up and they're watching. Fall down and they'll close in. They're that way. You can tell.

When Jewel had gone three streets east and the bombardiering of his own blood was less diverting, he leaned against a phone booth to rest. He was trying to think, but he'd grown shy about reaching conclusions. His own thoughts seemed clumsy and weak, and ever having believed them to be snappy and strong had been his big mistake. He thought that now, and suspicion of his own brain was paralyzing him. He thumped at his head with bloodied hands, wondering whose side his mind was on, anyway!

Jewel pulled his hand away from the glass phone booth and saw that he'd left a palm print of blood. He raised his elbow and smeared the print, then was stunned to stillness when a lurking idea jumped his consciousness. It was the only thing to do that he'd come up with, and when his hand searched his pockets he found that he had some change. The phone book had not been ripped out of the booth, and this, too, seemed like a good omen.

Jewel found the number and dialed with shaky fingers.

On the sixth ring the phone was answered by a woman with a big-city tone.

"Kelly's Pool Hall, Kelly speakin'."

"What? Where is this?"

"Who you lookin' for, Bub?"

Jewel's free hand was disciplining his head by jerking at the hair.

"I got the number from the book! I'm tryin' to find Pete."

"Pete? Pete the snooker player? Sure, he's usually here, but not right now."

"Do you know where he lives?"

The woman's laughter made Jewel yearn for rural crossroads with small stores, polite women, and good-natured sheriffs who winked on Saturday nights.

"You moron," she said, finally. "He lives here."

"I dialed this number."

"Is this Cobb?"

Oh, no, Jewel thought.

"Why do you want to know?"

" 'Cause Pete the snooker player is lookin' for you, asshole. That's why." The woman paused, then made her voice solicitous. "Where're you from, anyway, Cobb?"

The sudden friendliness of her tone prodded Jewel toward nostalgia.

"A sweet little place called Willow Creek."

"Is that right? Well, there sure must be a lot of dumb motherfuckers come from around there, judgin' by you."

"Geez, lady," Jewel said in a pained voice. "What is it, anyhow? You don't even know me—why you gotta be so mean? I might be the spittin' image of your favorite uncle, you know?"

"Poor lambikins," she said. "I'm Peggy, Pete's woman, and I ain't friendly to nobody that's friendly with him."

"Oh. I'm not his friend, I'm just tryin' to find him, is all."

"Try the Catfish."

"The what?"

"The Catfish Bar. It's on Lafitte Street, by the river. He'll be there elbow-buffin' the rail, unless I'm wrong, which ain't likely."

The phone clicked in Jewel's ear but he still said thank you before hanging his end up.

15

Near the corner of Lafitte and Clay streets, Shade saw a small, murky man whom he recognized as Claude Lyons. Lyons was sitting on the hood of a dented Toyota parked in front of a white stone tenement stoop, drinking from a plastic quart of Tab.

Shade sat next to him, with his arms folded.

"How's it goin', Claude?"

Lyons raised his blunt face and almost smiled. His hair was dense brown and spongy, his body short and broad.

"Hey, Rene. You makin' what you call a canvass of the neighborhood, huh? I thought you'd come up in the world."

Shade nodded even though he didn't quite get it.

"Is she dead?" Lyons asked.

"Who?"

After a swig of sugar-free, Lyons glumly faced Shade.

"It was the coons, I heard. I thought that shit had died down. If she's dead, that is. You tell me."

"What're you talking about, Claude?"

"The girl over on Voltaire that the coons shot." Lyons rested a hand on Shade's arm and leaned toward him. "You can tell me — is it true she was preg-o?"

"Where was this?"

"Just down Voltaire, man. You been gone fishin', or what? Little while ago a busload of coons come down and murdered a pregnant girl over there. Shot her through the baby's head, killed 'em both."

"Are you sure of this?"

"I heard it from Leo at the grocery."

"I better get over there."

"No kiddin', man," Lyons said. "And believe you me, Rene — ain't nobody happy about this shit comin' round again. I thought we'd settled it."

Shade walked quickly toward Voltaire Street, his senses pitched for weirdness, for clearly ominous coincidences were occurring. There was more shooting going on in a shorter span of time than Saint Bruno had tolerated since Auguste Beaurain had swept Frogtown clean of conspiratorial St. Louis dagos back in 1967. And *that* combat had had a mutant sense of civic pride about it that the present carnage lacked entirely.

The bored sweaters from the Chalk & Stroke were still on the sidewalk assessing the merits of the action across the street. They stood there in somber clots, the slack-lipped recorders of neighborhood legend, absorbing it all for improved retellings, countless. Shade walked through them and heard several angry voices speak of revenge.

Two uniformed cops were at the narrow door that led upstairs from between Connie's Hair Salon and the Olde Frenchtown Antique Shop.

As Shade approached, How Blanchette came down the

stairs. He began to shake his head when he saw Shade. He held his meaty hands to the sky.

"Shade, I been lookin' for you. Baby, somethin' is goin' on, and, like, we don't know what it is."

"What happened here? Guy over on Lafitte stopped me and said a woman got wasted over here."

"Nah," Blanchette said.

"By blacks."

"That part is makin' the rounds accurate. But the girl, a little spotted panty-type farm girl, with tits like your head, she's not gonna die. Blood all over her, but she's not really hurt that bad."

Shade pointed upstairs.

"Anything to see?"

"Blood. A guitar. Some cold fish sticks."

"Hunh."

"The girl, you want to know who she is?"

"Tell me who she is, How."

"Okay. Name's Susan Magruder. She's better known as the old lady of a plowboy hard-ass named Jewel Cobb." Blanchette chuckled. "Now, from the name you might figure him for an Afro-Sheen sort of guy, but you'd be wrong. Actually he's about twenty, with — and I think you'll find this interestin' — no visible means of support and a glob of blond hair that he piles up like a sort of Casper the Ghost Elvis."

It was no surprise.

"I had a feeling it might be a guy like that."

"Two or three black hoods come in here," Blanchette said, "and old blondie does a bellywhopper out the back window. He leaves Miss Tits to the dinges, and she hides herself in the john. Only one of the hoods seems to have heard of that trick, you know, and sends her a couple of goodwill messages through the door. Poor thing got some splinters driven into her shoulders, and a bullet chipped off a piece of thigh." Blanchette nodded at a blue-haired woman who was sitting in a police car. "She saw the white guy come out the back window and one of the guys who was tryin' to shoot him. She's sort of outraged, you know. An old-time neighborhood lady, you see, doesn't think it's right, smokes comin' down here to kill a white guy, even a stranger."

Although night was now nearly full-fledged, the heat of the day was lingering, hairlines dripped down faces, tempers went on the prowl, and relief was driving a hard bargain.

Shade spent several minutes talking to Mrs. Prouxl, the blue-haired lady. She told him that she'd just come out of the hair salon where not Connie but her assistant, Hank, had given her a new do that tended to draw an admirer's gaze up to her eyes, which were her best features, or at least so she'd always been convincingly told, when this blond, a boy, really, flew like a brick out of the second-story window and an eyelash later one of our equals under the law stuck his burr-head out the same window and tried to kill him for no reason. How could there be a reason for that? The white boy seemed to be bleeding, too, although from a bullet or what she couldn't say, and the whole ordeal just made her glad she was closin' in on gettin' called home, because in her day it just never could've happened, and if that was what modern life was going to be like, she'd rather switch channels in a very big way.

Shade thanked her so profusely that he felt just a little bit ashamed. He then rejoined Blanchette.

"It doesn't make any sense yet," Shade said. "But it's startin' to add up."

"Uh-huh." Blanchette sucked on his lips thoughtfully. "Crane and this Cobb kid hooks up easy. Now, is all this hooked to Alvin Rankin, too?"

"What do you think?"

"I think yes."

"Me, too." Shade watched as Mrs. Prouxl walked away, being queried by a couple of the spectators from across the street. She held her purse to her navel and didn't turn her head to her questioners.

"Grandma gave me some ideas. I'm going to check the alley."

"We already did that."

"I'll do it again. Make sure."

"Whatever makes you happy. Should I wait on you?"

"No."

The alley was a pothole with a few shovels of gravel thrown on it, and situated as it was, to the rear of ramshackle Voltaire Street, it offered a wonderful view of nothing wonderful. The garbage bins behind the hair salon smelled of permanent solution and a broken vial of eau de something or other unlikely.

The shattered window that Jewel had squirreled through was illuminated by a naked bulb in the apartment. Shade could see the jagged frame of glass that he would have had to slice himself on. The drop to the alley was not deadly, but the kid could easily be hurt by it.

He followed the alley to its southern exit, then turned left and crouched beneath the well-lit window of a doughnut shop and inspected the sidewalk. Still in a crouch he duck-walked in the pastry-bullied air, drawing a few interested glances from passersby. Then he saw what he sought. He dabbed a finger into the moist evidence and raised it to the light. Blood.

The trail of claret, although indistinct and occasional, could be followed with only minor hesitations. Shade hung with it across streets and around chancy corners, until he came to a telephone booth with a bloody payoff smeared at chest height. He looked in the booth but found only a closed phone book and extra flecks of blood. He knew that if the seepage did not stop soon Jewel Cobb must weaken. Of course the kid could find a taxi or a friend and disappear, Shade thought, but for now this trail was all there was to go on.

One block later good luck ran out and the trail disappeared. It was at the corner of Rousseau and Clay, but catty-cornered to Lafitte and an alley. The kid could've gone any of a dozen directions from here, and with no telltale drips it was impossible to follow.

Shade leaned against a lamppole and took what he had planned to be a healthy suck of night air, but turned out to be a greedy toke of stench. The weather was condensing the river, rotting it in its own broth. Shade made a face, then sniffed his shirt and made the same face again, only better.

The Catfish Bar was only a block away on Lafitte, and Shade, having decided that his sleuthery would be enhanced by the input of a couple of tall cool ones, figured the Cobb kid might've gone that refreshing direction as well as any other.

He passed his mother's poolroom and his own apartment. He halted to look in the window and saw that the tables were being put to good use and his mother was sitting on her stool smoking a long black cigarette. This had been home for most of memory but not all of it. The Shades had once lived in a house two streets up, with a dog-run yard and a cement basement, until the early morning Daddy John X. had laid the soul-search conclusion on Mama that his true self, his *real* true self, was a river-rambling man who frankly knew more than one doll and even more than one was no good if the mix was not kept sassy. So he wasn't leaving over no other woman but because of *women* who are an animal fact, so don't think shitty of him 'cause what he's got honestly is a problem that he ought to work out on his own, don't you see. But he *will* send money, sure, whenever that smile-yellow nine ball staggers in on the break. That had been twenty years before, and on the evidence, modern nine balls must have been glued to the felt.

Shade stood looking in the window for a moment more, then walked on.

When he entered the Catfish he thought his brother might give him a hard time. He was prepared for tension. He sat himself on a stool until Tip noticed him. There was a second of deadpan hesitation, then Tip smiled.

"Hey, Rene, how you doin'?"

"Hot," Shade said. He looked at his brother's broad, tough-guy face and saw friendliness. Odd. For even when Tip was full of joy he tended to scowl, and now he was doing a thick-necked, pockfaced parody of the Mona Lisa. "This town has busted loose."

"Yeah," Tip agreed. "I been hearin' about it." He shrugged. "It's time, I guess. Things have to go crazy every few years, you know, just so somebody can step in and put it all back in line."

"The bartender's view of life," Shade said. "Give me a draw."

As Tip went to get the beer, Shade turned to face the room. There was a total absence of blonds, let alone one who impersonated Elvis. In the corner there was a table of shot-and-beer locals who'd gotten newscaster haircuts and put on suits that were already smirkingly behind the tide of fashion, talking loudly about having to settle down and get *real* jobs, and ordering practice martinis. They laughed so much it was obvious that real jobs were not threateningly close at hand.

Bonne chance in the executive suite, Shade thought. But keep your shovels scraped, boys, and don't lose those double-thick leather work gloves.

Tip sat the beer in front of Shade. He turned and drank heartily. He could not afford to waste time, but the beer was uplifting and no sense being tight-assed about a brew or two.

"Hungry, li'l blood?"

"Not really," Shade said. "I could eat a sandwich."

"No problem."

Tip went through a swinging door into the kitchen as Shade watched. Again he found himself bemused by the apologetic attitude of big Tip.

When Tip came back out of the kitchen he turned and watched the door close before carrying the sandwich to Shade.

"Plenty of horseradish on it," he said. There was an uncertain tightness about his face. "The way you like it."

"Merci."

Tip glanced toward the kitchen door. Shade caught the glance and he thought nothing of it, but immediately it happened again and his spine sort of itched and his shoulders felt heavy.

"Expecting somebody?" he asked.

"Hunh? Oh, shit no. I was thinkin' maybe I should knock a hole in the wall there, so's you could watch the cook."

"Sure."

Mike Rondeau, a tall drink of a man sloshed into a squat glass, with a belt that could double as a lasso and a volume of ambitious lies that he called his life, came in the door and laughed.

"The Shade brothers," he said. "I had a feelin' I'd bump into you."

"This is where I work." Tip said. "Does that make you a prophet, that you found me here?"

"Oh, ho," Rondeau said to Shade, "you can always count on *him* for bad temper."

"Usually," Shade replied, then thought, yes, usually.

"What'll you have, Slim?" Tip asked.

"Do you have any carrot juice, perhaps?" the solemn-faced Rondeau asked.

"Sure, but not fresh. We have frozen."

"Ah," said Rondeau. "In that case make it a double rye with a beer back." He turned to Shade, winked, then ran a hand across his thin patch of white hair. "Have to nurse the old timekeeper."

"Yeah," Shade said. "I heard you had a heart attack."

"Just a little four-rounder on the backside of the heart. I got the decision."

Knowing that Rondeau was self-employed as a plumber – gambler – widow-lover, Shade said, "Must make business tough."

"I don't walk as fast, that's all. But when you win you can stroll, and when you lose — what's the hurry?"

Tip sat the drinks down and collected the money.

Shade caught Tip eyeballing the kitchen door again.

After a sip of rye and a follow-up of beer, Rondeau said, "Saw you boyses' daddy down in Cairo a week ago. Went down there to play some stud with a beaner philanthropist called Baroja who never showed. Ended up in a six-table joint by the river watchin' Little Egyptians shoot nine ball for quarters when in walks old John X. himself. My favorite man. Had a coat on that was green and glistened like he'd hooked it up off the bottom of the river and cut the gills out for arm-holes. Flashy, you know, in a way only a shithouse Mick could think was flashy."

Tip and Shade looked at each other, then turned away. Both felt dumped by their father, and despite the years alone, neither wanted to be.

"I'll have another," Rondeau said, rapping his empty glass. "He paid for my trip, plus some wingding dough. He got into a little nine-ball action with a fella called Dickie Venice, who's from New York and hasn't got any eyelids. His eyes're always open and you wonder why they don't dry out and crack but they don't. Looks like a cue-ball goldfish, this Venice fella does, but with a silky stroke, you know. Really smooth. I hung back and laid off of John X. at nine ball, then backed him to the limit when they switched to one-pocket. Got to be a fool not to bet him in one-pocket."

Tip slid the fresh drinks to him.

"He mention comin' up to see us?" He and Shade were both a bit weak when it came to John X., and wished they weren't because then they could show the old man their backs forever, but he was a hard man to do that to. "He say anything about us?"

"Let me think," Rondeau said. He raised his drink and took a bird-beak dip into it. "No, not really," he said in a soft tone. "See, he had some dates with him." He looked at the brothers, who both looked elsewhere. "Probably didn't seem like the time for family chat, you know. Couple of escaped wives on his arms, he wouldn't talk about birthdays and graduations, most likely."

"Escaped wives," Shade said. "He's good at escaping wives."

"He's still married to our mother," Tip said. "The prick. He should at least ask about her, don't you think? In between games when the balls are bein' racked, he could maybe ask, 'How's Monique doin' these days?' or something'."

"That's a sweet sentiment," Rondeau said. "But it's askin' a lot of the guy, under the circumstances."

There was a momentary silence, then the kitchen door swung open and a man with fingers of gray running through his brown hair came out. He walked briskly to a table where a lone beer had been left.

Shade knew he knew the man, but the name was not coming to him.

Tip patted his arm.

"How about another one?"

"I might could drink another."

It's Ledoux, Shade thought. He watched the man drink his beer. Yeah, Ledoux, Pat or Paul or Pete. A character, too, with several priors.

The table of double-breasted unemployed who'd been drinking martinis to acclimate themselves to higher-life beverages, but who still had that underbelly pride, which fears selling out, were herding on stiff Florsheims toward the door, their voices raised in lopsided harmony.

There was a twitch beneath Tip's eye, Shade noticed, and he seemed to be reining hard on his head to keep from looking at Ledoux.

As Shade hoisted his brew he felt Ledoux walk behind him. He watched Tip. Tip's eyes rose for the length of a wink, then lowered like a phantom nod. Shade turned to watch Ledoux go out the door.

The itch was back in Shade's spine, along with the heaviness of shoulder and shot-in-the-dark suspicions. After another contemplative sip of beer he scooted off the stool and went toward the kitchen.

"What?" Tip asked. "Hey, man!"

Shade pushed the door open. The grill was off and a kettle of stew steamed on the range. The floor was wet with fresh mopping and the backdoor was open to the screen. Russ Poncelet, looking institutional in his all-white ensemble, was rubbing a rag along the sides of the steel cooler.

Shade stepped into the room, looking for anything solid to confirm his suspicions.

Tip leaned in the doorway.

"What're you doin'?"

"Just lookin'."

There was nothing strongly out of place in the room.

"Can't get us on cleanliness," Poncelet said. "I just gave it a washing down. You could eat off the floor safer than usin' your fingers. Pine-Sol."

Shade felt ridiculous but not ashamed, and spun on his heels. He pushed past Tip.

"You're a pain in the fuckin' ass," Tip said as Shade went to the exit. "You're a punchy fuckin' weirdo sometimes, you know that? You should've ducked once in a while."

Outside in the pungent night, Shade sprinted around the corner to the parking lot. The white dust shone in the moonlight and small scudding wisps of it lingered in the air.

He's gone, Shade thought. Maybe it was just as well, for what had he really planned to do? Say, "Man, you make my spine itch, what is it," or what? It could've been silly.

But he didn't really think so.

16

Saint Joseph's Hospital served the maimed and mauled on the B side of the city. Pan Fry, Frogtown, and the south side kept the emergency room relevant and made it a frequent meeting place.

The room itself looked like a bowling alley that had missed a payment on its lanes. Lots of faded plastic chairs in muted colors, flaking green paint on the walls, with only one bright light and that directly above the nurse's desk.

When Shade entered, a young tattooed man with skin taut as rice paper, a showy flattop, and an incredible amount of patience was standing at the desk holding a Baggie up.

"It's my thumb, lady. It flew past the toolbox but I found it. I don't know how long it'll keep."

Shade saw that one of the man's hands was knotted by a sky-blue towel that had recently become two-toned.

"It hurts like hell, lady."

"You're not goin' to die," the nurse said. "That means you have to wait."

"Lady, my thumb gets room temperature, I'm fucked. Damn, it hurts!"

Shade walked on, cutting through the building to the main desk on the far side. Once there, he was given the room number and got on the elevator. He got off on the fourth floor. It was getting late in the shift, and the nurses' uniforms had lost their crispness. The floors were waxed to brightness and the air conditioning was chilling.

There was a uniformed officer in front of room 446. Shade showed him his shield and was admitted to the room.

Suze was awake, propped up in bed. There were bandages on her shoulder, neck, and thigh. Her skin was pale as steam, and her hair was matted into a straggly clump.

"I'm Detective Shade, Miss Magruder. We need to talk."

"Well," she said, her voice made meek by painkillers, "I already talked to the fat guy."

"This is different."

Suze looked at Shade appraisingly, then sat up straighter in bed.

"Okey-dokey. But keep the fat guy away, will you?"

"I'll try to. Why do you think this happened?"

"Is Jewel okay? Have you found him?"

"No."

"He's dead, ain't he?"

"We don't know that. I don't believe he is."

"He will be."

"You're sure they wanted to kill him? Not just scare him?"

Suze's eyes widened.

"Oh, no," she said, shaking her head. "These was *real* sincere people. They're gonna kill him."

"What's Jewel's business up here? You and him, you're not from around here."

"No. No we ain't from nowhere's around here." She spoke in a resigned tone. "We come up here for the better opportunities. Jewel's got a cousin out in one of these buildings around here."

"Is that right. What's his cousin's name?"

"Duncan."

"Duncan Cobb?"

"Sure. That family is considered trash in other places just 'cause they're rowdy."

Shade sat at the foot of the bed and smiled.

"They get blamed for a lot of things?"

"Just about everything short of weather. They usually did it, too, but you can't just *know* they done it, you have to *prove* it on 'em. So they don't stop. Real rowdy folks."

"Look, I have a better chance of helping Jewel if I know what he's involved in. What is he into?"

"Look, mister, I can't say. Jewel, he never told me anything I wanted to know." She was beginning to quaver but not out of control. "He's not that sweet of a guy but I love him in that bulldog way, you know. Pup nips you, you still feed it. We had some fun, me and him. We used to smoke a joint and drink some beer — romp around the woods and stuff. Get naked in a pond when the days are that way. We might find a lost shoat once in a while and gig it with a spit over our campfire — but, shoot. That's just livin'. Only Jewel said you have to get serious sometime. I reckon he did, too."

"It looks like it," Shade said. "Could you recognize the men who shot you?"

"I already told the fat guy that I couldn't. I hardly even saw 'em. Alls I know is, they come in like the real thing, mister. There wasn't nothin' TV about it."

141

After thanking Suze, and wishing her well, Shade left the hospital intent upon checking out this rowdy relative, Duncan Cobb.

It was four hot blocks to his own apartment. The light was still on downstairs and he could see that there was some straight pool education going on. He went up the back stairs to his apartment.

He opened his refrigerator and found a frigid can of Stag beer buried behind the wheat germ jar. He plopped on the couch and opened the brew, then reached for the telephone. He called How Blanchette at the station.

"Blanchette."

"This is Shade. I followed this Cobb kid but I couldn't find him. He's got a cousin, though, and we ought to check him out, I think."

"I know," Blanchette said. "Duncan Cobb, twenty-nine, five-nine, one eighty. Two priors, both misdemeanors. Busted for assault seven years ago, and he got popped with fightin' spurs at a raided cockfight about three months ago. Paid a fine."

"Doesn't sound like a desperado, exactly."

"No, but he works for Micheaux Construction — find that interestin'?"

"Steve Roque."

"Yes. And Pete Ledoux."

"Pete Ledoux," Shade said, verging on a revelatory quake. "I tell you what, I just saw Ledoux. I lost the kid but ran into Ledoux at the Catfish."

"Ledoux's one of those swampfrogs, lives out on Tecumseh Road, there, just before you sink into the Marais du Croche. Someone should go visitin', I think."

"I'm going to."

"But be careful. Pete Ledoux's the sort of guy who, if he

saw a Mack truck comin' in on him he'd just tuck his chin behind his shoulder and double up on his hooks, you know. Not your basic candy-ass, that guy."

"I'll be on my best behavior."

"Also," Blanchette's voice dropped to a conspiratorial whisper. "A Miss Webb called for you. Didn't leave a message, and I'm no psychiatrist, but I *do* think I know what she wants."

"Yeah, well save it for when you're alone, your guesses about what she wants."

"Just tryin' to help a buddy, buddy."

"Give me Duncan Cobb's address," Shade said. "I think I'll fire up my Nova and drop in on him, too."

"You do that. He lives at 1205 Twelfth Street," Blanchette said. "I got to go to the mayor's office and explain why his town is explodin'. I think I'll blame it on the weather."

17

The dark of the nighttime streets was carved by lights of many hues and varying constancies; the red from the Boy O Boy Chicken Shack was a quick flick of the wrist and the green from Johnny's Shamrock a steady stab, while the rainbow in Irving's Cleaners was a slight but constant scrape. Streetlights and porch lights helped to slice away at the blackness, but the night had heart and stood up under it all well.

Powers Jones sat in the back seat of his own red Thunderbird, for the Ford wagon had been abandoned. Benny, his too-cool-to-be-true driver, and Lewis Brown were in the front seat. Lewis had been given the start over young Thomas, who was holed up in a double-locked room trying to convince himself that the terrible shaking of his limbs was a result of his having skipped supper.

"This man the cousin," Powers said as they circled the

block. "Our voice on the cops says he works for Froghead Ledoux, too. *He* the one started this."

"Don't need to hear about it," Lewis said, jabbing his chin upward. "I don't remember nothin' I never heard, you see."

Lewis was a dreadlocked thirty-year-old with a vest of pudge and ganja-inspired eyes. Despite the flab and his short stature, he did not give an impression of softness.

"Cool," Powers said. "You solid ice."

On the next circuit Benny pulled over and parked near Johnny's Shamrock.

The window of the bar was wriggling with the jocular hoistings of the hard-drinking patrons. Mugs of Guinness, Irish hats, and cigars bobbed in the haze of blue smoke and high-tenor bullshit.

"He'll be in there," Powers pointed out. "Gettin' a bag on like they always do. They got to be lit to work. Me, I get lit after."

"Mmm-hmm," Lewis agreed. "They breed 'em too gentle for the life anymore."

"That is true. Except for them Frogs."

"You right. You are right about that. Why *is* that?"

Power stroked his beard thoughtfully.

"They too stubby for sports and too lazy to work," he said with some wistfulness. "But they need that prestige, so they *can* be rugged."

"Everybody needs that," Benny said, speaking for the first time in hours. Benny had been an assistant librarian at the Boonville Reformatory for one-to-three and had garnered some sophistication about the world. "Chinese, A-rabs, Texans — they all about the same when you come right down to it, far as that prestige thing goes."

"That so?" Powers responded. "You know, you talkin' too much, Benny. Why'n't you eat another down, huh?"

145

"Downs," Lewis said. "This boy on downs?"

"I can still drive," Benny said. "I ain't scared of nothin'."

"On the road? Can you drive on the road?" Lewis asked. "That's a myth, that gettin' down. Drugs are for gettin' high, man, not that down like you dead shit."

Powers thumped his fist against the seat back, forcefully redirecting the conversation.

"Hey — that's him. I seen him before around town. That is him for certain."

Duncan Cobb was standing on the sidewalk in front of the Shamrock, making rude gestures into the window and laughing Gaelically. Several fingers responded with raps on the glass, bidding him carnal farewell. He laughed, then began to walk home with a Guinness lilt in his step.

"You get up ahead of the man," Powers said to Lewis. "We can't be messin' up on this one, neither."

In his yellow shirt and white pants, with the eye-catching roll to his walk, Duncan was suicidally luminescent. He paused to light a cigarette, but since he smoked only when he was drunk he found the process taxing his coordination. As he scratched a match he heard footsteps and looked up to see one of his pet peeves blocking the sidewalk.

"You seen my mama?" Lewis asked him gruffly.

"This is Twelfth Street, bro," Duncan said. He dropped the cigarette and matches, then shifted his weight more or less into punching balance. "I ain't even polite on Twelfth Street."

Lewis backed up half a step and tried to look intrigued.

"I'm lookin' for my mama 'cause I'm in a blue funk," he said, then woefully wagged his dreadlocked head. "When I feel this a way, see, my mama, she lets me beat on her till *I* feel happy again."

"I ain't your Ubangi mama, bro."

As swift as a gnat in the eye, a pistol appeared at Duncan's side with Powers Jones backing it up. Duncan turned to face down the barrel.

"But you'll do, motherfucker," Lewis said, then professionally punted him in the balls.

The grit on the floorboards had begun to rub Duncan's face raw. There was a boot on his head and nausea in his gut. He was confused and bruised and full of wonder.

"This is uncalled for," he said, the blare of the car radio overriding his words. Someone turned the sound up and an old Jackson Five tune about young love blasted in the air.

The car careened and swayed through a mystery of streets, then came to a halt. Duncan had no idea where he was. His arms were grasped and he was rudely extracted from the car. Once outside he saw that they were in Frechette Park, going up the walkway to the Boys Club. They used the rear, unlighted entrance.

"I don't know what this is," Duncan said. "I really don't. I certainly don't. It's uncalled for. You got the wrong man."

"You ain't no man. You a shitpile with feet."

The heavy metal door was held open by a blurred figure in the shadows. Duncan was shoved inside. The blur handed a wad of keys to Powers and told him to drop them by later.

The corridor was dark but Duncan was pushed along at an unkind pace, his body moving uncertainly, awkwardly tensing for a blind collision at any moment. If he'd known his way around he might have tried running, but he didn't and knew it, and they did. He knew that, too.

Soon they came to a door. There was a blade of light coming from the bottom gap.

"Open it," Lewis said.

Duncan turned to the voice. There seemed to be three of them: the plugged-in one with the charged hair and the understanding mama; the bearded one with the gun; and one who breathed real loud.

He hesitated at the door and received a jolt in the kidney. "Now, motherfucker!"

He opened the door and entered the bright room. There were thick quiltlike pads on the floor. Parallel bars and a pommel horse were in the center of the room.

Sitting on the horse was a smorgasbord portion of bad, bad luck, eyeballing him.

The no-blarney menace stood and clasped his hands politely.

"My name is Sundown Phillips — you've heard of me?"

"Well," Duncan said, "I think maybe I have. This is, this is uncalled for, man."

"We'll see." Sundown motioned to a chair near the horse. "Have yourself a rest."

Duncan sat and looked up at his host who sort of thunderclouded over him.

"I been around the block many a time, Mr. Cobb, and I've gained a certain *regard* from the people on the street."

"I've heard that," Duncan said. "I've heard folks, many people, say things of you, you know, man, with a high regard. High regard."

Sundown flared his lips and beamed toothily.

"That's nice. I like to hear that. I know lots of folks consider me to be kind of sinister, but I just think I been lucky."

Duncan agreed.

"I never knew nothin' bad about you, man."

After a smiley pause Sundown hunkered down to Duncan's level. He nodded and put a fracas-gnarled hand on Duncan's knee. He then wagged a finger in his face.

148

"There's a lot of things goin' on here," Sundown said, the smooth con disappearing from his voice and a tone that suggested razor fights and happiness *about* razor fights replacing it. "And you could fill me in on it."

"What? What do you mean?"

"Like your blood, Jewel, who been goin' around town dealin' out brothers."

"Oh."

Benny, who'd been doing a circular nod-walk inspecting things, suddenly began to kick at a locked door. His red platform shoes went skidding across the buffed floor, but he kept up the attack with a naked heel. The booms rattled in the room but the door stood firm.

Powers moved toward him.

"Benny, what the fuck you doin'?"

Benny turned, a look of stoned perseverance on his face. His speech was slow.

"That's where they keep the Ping-Pong balls," he said. "You got to post a quarter bond to use one. Every time. I always wanted to bust in there. This my chance."

With a look of nervous consternation on his face, Lewis said, "I ain't ever workin' with that boy again. Make sure he forgets all about me, hear?"

"Benny, go outside," Sundown said evenly. He watched Benny leave, then patted Duncan's knee and wagged the finger again. "I think you can tell me just about all I want to know, Cobb. And, just for fun" — he smiled widely — "lets us *pretend* that your *life* depends on it."

A look of timid shrewdness came into Duncan's eyes, as if he knew in advance that his lies would be inadequate, but he had to take the chance of telling them. He looked from face to face in the room and found little comfort in the various expressions.

149

"I don't know what you mean, man. I really don't."

Sundown curled his lips, sighed, then nodded sadly.

"Lewis — show him what I mean."

Lewis Brown, a man who found a personal music in the moans of others, stepped up to Duncan.

"I want you to know," he said softly, "that I *like* your attitude. I really do. But I *am* gonna have *fun* changin' it."

When Duncan could focus again he realized that he was hanging upside down, his wrists and ankles lashed to the parallel bars. His teeth felt mushy and his arms felt ingrown. There was a new arrangement with his eyes, one opened and one wouldn't.

His whole life seemed like a cramp now.

"He's back," Powers said. "The eye on the fresh side of his head fluttered up."

Sundown crouched toward Duncan's loyal eye. His face was stern and not bored.

"It ain't goin' to get better," he said. There was a dull aloofness to Duncan's arms, and extra knobs at his shoulders where bones had been freed from sockets. Purple and blue welts swathed his face, leaving just the one eye bare.

"Ohh," he groaned. "Ohh, Jesus. I'm not. I'm not Jewel. Man! Ohh!"

Sundown raised one loglike leg and rested his toe in the soft space between shoulder and arm.

"Man, I know you're in it with him," Sundown said. "And must be Pete Ledoux is in it, too. And Ledoux, he don't do *too much* without Steve Roque givin' the okay on it." He prodded with his toe and the interviewee writhed. "You just meat to them, Cobb. I like you. And I'm the only man can help you right now."

"Ohh, I just don't know, man!"

150

After a reflective pause, Sundown leaned his full weight behind his probing foot, and there was a brief, high-note scream, then blackout silence.

On his next return to this world, Duncan Cobb, oldest son, faithless cousin, cautious lover, and pal of killers, awoke infused with the lucidity born of no escape, and a mortal dose of honesty.

He spoke in spasms, his body swaying in its moor, his voice leached of emphasis. All recollections were becoming equal.

"Music Center," he said. "The nigger who was elected — he was a businessman. Ohh."

"Alvin Rankin?"

"Him. Oh, him. He did business. He shopped around. We bought the Music Center job. Thousands, maybe. Thousands in it."

"No, you wrong," Sundown said. "*I* got the Music Center."

"He shopped it twice. Ahh. We done deals with him before you. Cut us out when the bread gets, ahh, long."

"Who the fuck hit him?"

"Ohh." A gurgling sound like an afterlife chuckle came from Duncan's throat. "Guh, guh. Crane. Your boy. Crane."

"No."

"Guh, guh. Ohh. Had him by the nuts. Juice was eatin' him up. Way in the hole to us. Had kids, too. Ahh. Way. Way in the hole."

"The hit squared him up, huh?"

"Guh, guh, guh."

Sundown rested on the pommel horse, a stunned sag to his posture.

"Alvin died over this? I would've stepped out to keep him

from bein' whacked over this, for God's sake. It ain't worth it. I could've straightened it out later."

"Oh."

"Steve Roque is behind this."

Sundown turned to Powers and Lewis, who'd pulled the bottom bench of the bleachers out and were squatting there, elbows on knees, chins in hands. His brows clenched into a serious V and his fists balled.

"There some nefarious deeds goin' on," he said. He saw the chop-fallen look on his associates' faces. "That means dark and shitty stuff."

"We equal to it," Powers Jones said, jumping up. "They get it started, but we *more* than equal to it."

"Of course," Sundown said, dryly. "You've proved that."

Lewis gestured at the dangling Duncan.

"What about this boy?"

Slowly Sundown turned his gaze on his reluctant oracle. Duncan wiggled his body so that he could see, with his one now-wide open eye, Sundown's face.

"Well, we got to do the right thing by this boy," Sundown said. "The *right* thing."

Duncan's neck relaxed and his head flopped back gratefully.

"Uh-huh," Lewis said. "Naturally we'll do the right thing by him."

"Then after that," Powers interjected, "should we dump him in the river?"

Sundown raised his arms and shrugged.

"What else? Carp got to eat, too."

Now comprehension made Duncan rigid, and he let his important eye flap shut, choosing not to view the most glamorous occurrence, the straight-razor finale, to this his gaudy, but already forgotten, life.

152

18

The dock was all in darkness, even the full moon's rays being blocked by the high loom of nearby trees. Jewel Cobb lay on his back staring up, listening to the night sounds of the river and the Marais du Croche beyond. Owls hooted, and the river sidled up to the dock with wet whispers. Something snapped a branch on the other side and the sharp note of the crack wafted across the water. He sat up.

He'd been waiting for most of an hour. It had taken him fifteen minutes to sneak there from the kitchen of the Catfish. Ledoux had inspected the cuts on his side and said, "You cut bad, mon ami. Get up to my place and we'll take care of you. Watch out for niggers."

All Jewel could think of as he slinked along the dirt lane that led upriver was "buenas noches" and "hasta luego," for he was of the opinion that it was Mexico for him. But he didn't speak Mex. He could get patched up, though, then smuggle on downriver to some place with an airport and get to greaseball country where the laws were silly and you just paid off for anything you done like it was a traffic ticket. Yup, that'd be the place to cool out.

There was a splash nearby, a warning splash, a splash of something that might be big enough to come up on land with its mouth open. Jewel looked to where the sound had come from but couldn't see anything.

The bandages on his sides were coming loose. The big pock-faced guy in the kitchen had been nervous, in a hurry, and Ledoux hadn't really taped him up good. It wasn't that much pain, or blood, anymore, but it'd still be better if Pete showed up, 'cause he was getting dog tired. He could relax, just get in the boat and relax, once Pete came home and took charge.

That'd be the ticket.

Yeah.

When Pete Ledoux entered his house he saw a cigarette glowing near the window.

"Peggy?" he said.

"Where's the car?" she asked.

"Down the road. My boy get here?"

"I told him to wait on the dock. He's a puppy. He's just layin' there."

"Good."

"You could hear him if he walked," she said. "I'm goin' to have a beer — want one?"

"Nah." Ledoux went into the bedroom as Peggy opened a beer. When he came back out he carried a Remington 876 shotgun. "Where're my shells?"

"Am I supposed to know?" Peggy asked. She swigged half a

beer and wiped her mouth with her hand. "You used some when you splattered that gar, whenever that was."

"I know the plastic ones are on top of the fridge."

"That's right," she said. She reached up and brought down a tattered box of plastic twelve-gauge shells.

"No," Ledoux said. "Keep 'em, they're for shit. Cheap-ass shells."

Peggy finished her beer and tossed the empty into the trash.

"You're *such* a man, Petey. Why the hell don't you just club the snotnose to death?"

Ledoux shook his head.

"He's only a boy," he said. "That means energy. It could be too messy. Or he might get away."

"Use the plastic shells, then."

"I guess I have to." He waved his hand in Peggy's face. "If you kept decent house I could find the good shells. Can't find shit around here."

"Aw, Petey, honey — if I kept house you'd lose respect for me. Respect's important to a marriage."

"My gun jams with cheapshit shells I'm goin' to slap your face, 'cause it'll be your fault."

"Everything always is," Peggy said, and opened the fridge for another beer.

After a grunt of dissatisfaction, Ledoux took the plastic shells and grimly stepped out the door.

The footsteps came like drumbeats down the suspended runway to the dock.

Jewel stood up.

"Pete?"

The steps came closer.

"Pete?" Jewel trembled, then jumped back. "Hey, man! What's with the piece, huh?"

155

"Relax, Cobb," Ledoux said as he walked past him. "Keep your fuckin' head on straight." There was a boat with an outboard motor tied up to one of the dock pillars. Ledoux stepped into the boat, steadying himself with a hand on the pillar. He laid the shotgun on the dock. "See if I can get this sucker started."

"Uh-huh. Where're we goin'?"

"Cabin I got, over there." Ledoux pointed toward the swamp. "In a couple of days we'll go to the other side. A guy'll pick you up there. Nobody'll know."

"Can I send a message to my girl?"

"Oh, hell yes, you peckerwood idiot. Send her a message and a fuckin' map, why not, so's she can bring you some sugar cookies and another squad of niggers with guns. Hell yes."

Jewel backed off.

"It don't matter," he said.

The engine kicked over easily and rattled to life.

"Mon Dieu," Ledoux said. "Runs like a tee."

Ledoux stepped back onto the dock and picked up the shotgun. He held it loosely by the trigger guard.

"Go on and get in. Be careful you don't tip it over."

As Jewel stepped into the boat Ledoux jacked a shell into the chamber. Jewel collapsed to the boat bench.

"Sorry, kid," Ledoux said. "You gotta go."

Jewel curled up in the bottom of the boat.

"I ain't gonna tell, man! I don't know nobody *to* tell!"

Ledoux wanted a head shot. The boat was wobbling and Jewel lurched with it. He pointed between Jewel's eyes and nodded, then pulled the trigger. Click. Nothing. He pumped another shell and the ejection slot stuck open.

"Damn!" Ledoux shouted, then quickly added, "You pass, kid. Duncan said you were cool as polar bear shit, and you really are. Lotta heart, kid."

"What the fuck?"

"Just checkin' your balls, Cobb. Enormous. Really. Now I feel like we can be partners."

"Man, don't do that shit with me!"

The engine was loud. Ledoux bent to Jewel for easier dialogue.

"I gotta run back up to the house, mon ami. Get us some grub. You like corned beef, I hope. You wait, huh? Then we'll be gone."

Jewel nodded slowly, his eyes never leaving his new partner's face.

Halfway to the house Ledoux heard the pitch of the motor shift and turned to see Jewel speeding off in the boat, pushing into the night.

He dropped the shotgun and kicked at it, spinning it off the runway.

"Goddamn fucking women!" he screamed.

It's all water and none of it's safe. Home was some kind of weak-hope shit, but better 'n this. Jewel tried to steer but he didn't know where to go. He headed for the trees, thinking that land must be near them.

Gonna kill that bacon-fat Duncan and his whole limb of the family tree. That'll be my payback.

The boat was run aground within minutes, ridden up on a spit of unexpected earth in the Marais du Croche.

Jewel Cobb sat on the boat bench, still and silent, waiting a long time before getting out. He gingerly tested the earth with his foot. It seemed he could walk on it, so he did, his heels sinking with each step.

19

As Rene Shade drove north on Tecumseh his thoughts were of change, the changes on the street. In his father's day, or so he'd been winkingly told, skull cracking was a sort of larkish after-mass sport, but using a knife was considered a sign of natural girlishness. But he was Irish. Shade's grandfather Blanqui, on the other hand, had never been without his hook-bladed linoleum cutter, and frequently wheezed cheap cigar breath while practicing pulling it from his pocket and opening it in one malevolent move. By the time of Shade's own sharp-toed shiny shoe period, knives were mundane and single-action pistols a sign of mature vision. And today, today it often seemed that any fifteen-year-old worth nodding to had at least shot *at* somebody with a secret Armalite. Violence had lost the personal touch, the pride had gone out of self-preservation, and mere chickenshit possibilities of im-proved technology replaced it.

Shade had gone looking for Duncan Cobb but with no success. He'd checked the address they had on him and prowled the corner tavern where it seemed no one had seen him, now or ever. So Shade was heading north to Pete Ledoux's. The headlights picked up the shock of weeds that flanked the lane and the water-filled gullies in between. There were no street signs out here, but mailboxes offered an occasional clue. Soon Shade found a lane and drove down it until his path was blocked by a black Pinto.

He parked and approached the house. He could see a light on inside. When he drew closer he saw the blue flicker of a television set.

He thumped on the porch door but no one answered. He let himself in, then knocked again at the interior door.

When the door opened he flipped his badge at the shape that stood behind it. His other hand grasped the butt of his thirty-eight.

"Detective Shade. Can I come in?"

The shape turned on a light. Her blond hair framed her face like crabgrass does flagstone. There were black highlighters beneath her eyes and a can of beer in her hand.

"Can I stop you?" she asked.

"No."

"Say no more," she replied and walked away from the door.

Shade followed her into the room. The television had a fuzzy picture and newspapers from barely remembered Sundays littered the furniture and floor. An intimidating load of dirty laundry was piled in one corner, and plates with entrenched yolks sat on the table.

"Cop a squat," Peggy said. "Just shove some shit off the chair, hunh."

Shade decided to sit on top of the newspapers in a rocking chair.

"Is Pete Ledoux here?"

"Not right now."

"You're Mrs. Ledoux?"

"Roughly," she said. "You know anything about TVs?"

"Not much."

"Too bad. I'm not much of a talker when the tube's on the blink like it is. I ain't a thumbsucker but I *do* need that tube, you know?"

"Where's Ledoux?"

"Brazil."

"Oh, yeah?"

"Not really," Peggy said. She drank some beer, then rested the can on her thigh, where it left damp circles. "It's one of my lies. Not too good, is it?"

She was still an attractive woman, Shade saw, beneath that sullen veneer of bloat.

"I've heard worse and I've heard better. You are in between."

Peggy shrugged.

"I'm not even really tryin'."

"Where is he?"

Peggy stared at the television.

"Now you tell me something," she said, pointing at the static warped screen, "that picture, there — is that Ted Koppel or Johnny Carson? Which is it?"

"You stump me," Shade said. "But I'm gettin' bored with it." Curiosity about how lazy one person could be drove Shade to check the set. He noticed that the screws holding the antenna wire were loose. "Got a screwdriver?"

"I don't know where. Can I get you a beer?"

"No thanks."

Shade pulled a dime from his pocket and used it in lieu of a screwdriver. The picture cleared immediately.

"Is that better?"

Peggy was attacking a fresh beer but took the time to look at the picture.

"Somewhat," she said. "It's somewhat better. Let me see that dime."

Shade handed it to her.

"Wouldn't Cobb fix it for you?"

"Who?"

Her face was calm. She bent over the television set and scraped the dime against the panel, then dropped it in her pocket.

"That's my dime."

She backed off, sluttishly coy.

"You have the prettiest blue eyes," she said. "Why don't we wrestle for it?"

"No thanks," Shade said. "Get yourself somethin' pretty, though."

She slumped back to the couch.

"Bashful," she said.

She caught Shade looking at the pile of laundry.

"Pete won't let me touch that," she said, then nodded. "It's a scientific experiment."

"Uh-huh."

"He's an evolutionist, you know. None of that Bible blather. He thinks you leave enough dirty T-shirts in a pile, sooner or later there'll be some bubblin' and gurglin' and a rack of Arrow shirts'll come foldin' out."

"Old Pete sounds like quite a guy."

"Oh, he is. He really is. Scientific mind, that guy." She stood and closed in on Shade. "It's my weakness. I'm just a sucker for scientists."

"That sounds pretty safe."

"You know what makes a kettle of water boil?" she asked,

sliding her leg between his and turning her tomatoey eyes up to him.

"Heat," he replied.

A look of viperine certainty came into her face, and her free hand dropped to his crotch.

"See," she said with a loll to her head, "you're sort of a scientist yourself."

"I thought I might qualify."

Someone began to knock on the screen door in banging combinations. Without waiting for an answer a tall man with an angry face and an overfed midsection came inside.

"Where'd your fuckin' old man go, Peg?" he asked. He looked at Shade and didn't seem impressed, then did a double take. "I know you. You used to be a boxer."

"Right."

The man snorted.

"Saw you get your clock cleaned a couple of times."

"Sure. Nobody seems to have seen the ones I won."

"Yeah, well, I seen you and you never showed me shit." He poked a finger at Peggy. "Your old man came down and took my boat. I don't like that. He didn't ask, he just took it."

"Our boatline snapped," Peggy said. She was looking at Shade. "He's tryin' to catch it before it drifts too far."

"Huh. I didn't see it float by. And I just come up here on my other boat and I seen runnin' lights *upriver* at the swamp."

Peggy's chin went south and she faced away.

Shade went to the phone on the table and began to dial.

"What in hell's goin' on?" the neighbor asked.

"Have a beer," Peggy said.

When Blanchette answered, Shade said, "It's me, How. Ledoux's in this thing. It's him. I'm at his place."

"You got him?"

"No. He's in a boat. I think Cobb is, too. They're over in the Marais du Croche. I'm going after them."

"Hey, be cool, comrade. That's a mess over there."

"You just get up here and back me up, How."

Shade dropped the phone back into the cradle, then looked out the window. He saw the running lights of a boat tied to the dock.

He approached the neighbor and flipped his badge.

"I'm goin' to need your boat. Police business."

"I don't think so," the big man said, then blocked the doorway. "Nobody's takin' my boat."

"I'm a cop."

"I don't fuckin' care if you're *six* cops, buddy. I'm Harlan Fontenot, that's *my* boat."

Shade feinted a right toward the jaw, and when the big man's hands went up he leaned into a left hook that sank deep into the mashed potatoes. The man sagged, and slumped to the floor.

Shade stepped around the man. "I just don't have the time."

He went out the door and ran down the walkway to the dock. He got into the boat and pulled away from the dock, trailing at least one killer into the swamp called the Marais du Croche.

20

The Marais du Croche was whorled with sloughs and mud rises like a gigantic fingerprint. It teased those who thought they knew it, and made a mockery of maps, as it changed with each heavy rain and was born anew with the floods of spring.

It had been years since Shade had been in the swamp. At the ducktail hairstyle and matching jackets stage of Frogtown adolescence the edges of the Crooked Swamp had provided a haven for queasy rites of passage. Chicken coops were erected there and called clubhouses, with blotched mattresses on the floor, surrounded by Stag beer cans, crushed by fresh virility, and empty mickeys of fruit-flavored vodka, dramatically pitched toward the corners. Unlikely magazine pages were taped to the walls and desperate girls acquired insurmountable local reputations there, on the mattresses, in the clean spots between the major stains. Shade had once felt that this was his turf, that he knew it well. But he knew he was a visitor to it now.

The moon was full and the sky had been dusted clean of clouds, so the half light of the bright orb was unobstructed. Shade circled in his borrowed craft, slowly searching the inlets and ditches for the other boats. The various waters flowed and ebbed and splashed and heaved, keeping up a constant fluidic murmur. Sometimes he could hear another boat but the sound was diffused by the swamp—one moment seeming to come from the main-coiled slough, and an instant later from downriver where the huge sandbars were.

The low arch of branches forced Shade to kneel as he steered the boat down sluggish tracts of bilious water. His hair was snatched at by swamp-privet strands, and the moonlight was no longer of use in such density. The water bubbled. Stinks that had been fermenting for lifetimes rose from the alluvial depths, then farted beneath his face. It was a rare, rich, meaningful stink, and not unpleasant to his nose.

He hadn't been here in a time that was too long. He felt that now.

To have a plan in a place that defied plans so completely was to embrace delusion, so Shade went where accidents took him and stayed alert for signs.

As one branch of swamp circled into another, taking him in toward the center, then drifting him back to the fringe, Shade hefted his pistol. He hoped to save a life, but he was awake to the possibilities and prepared also to take one if things fell that way.

This boy Cobb had the ways of a punk and a loser's heart, and Shade hoped not to kill him. Things could happen so many screwy ways, and half a lifetime ago he might, but for timidity or luck, have been in the same boat. He had always known that.

This is where Shade thought his life could make a difference. He was not guided by a total love of law, but he was more for it than against it, and this, he felt, made him reasonable. And that was the summit of his aspirations.

He hadn't heard the other motor for a long time when he saw a boat jumped up on a spit of land. The rotors of its engine had dug into the mud like frantic fingernails.

He pulled up to the spit and tied his bowline to the grounded boat. The beached craft was empty. There was a string of earth that led between the trees, deeper into the swamp.

The ribbon of mud was untraceable by sight, trailing into the gloom of undergrowth and woods — a mystery after twenty yards.

He decided to follow it.

Jewel Cobb soon decided that trying to get anywhere in this swamp was sort of childish. The next step was half the time into darkness, sinkhole or ditch, the rest of the time it was mud that gave way enough to goose your heart, then solided up. He'd fallen into the water twice. His shorts seemed full of coffee grounds and his asshole felt pounded with sand. There was ancient compost between his teeth and his boots squeaked like a third-grade violinist.

For a while Jewel had broken into a demented sprint, bouncing off trees, catching his boots in willow roots, stumbling, moaning, and kicking his feet high through the ditches, and laughing, propelled by some hopeless hilarity.

These could be the very last laughs coming to him from life as he'd made it, he knew, but that didn't make them worth much more.

Soon he just sat. There was a bullfrog chorus, gone silent at his approach, which quickly sized him for a chump and began to blat amphibian blues. Their tune made him feel less alone. But he couldn't relax. He nodded to the syncopation of the gut-bucket blats and tried to breathe quietly because telltale sound carried on the water and there was water everywhere.

Duncan, lard-faced cousin Duncan. Meet him again, someday sure, kick his butt around the block and piss on the bloody spots. Uh-huh.

Snakes, Jewel sensed them everywhere on the tangled floor. Limbs and slithery roots shadowed indistinct, all over. Anything could be a cottonmouth sleeping with a poison sac waiting to squirt the end of everything into your ankle veins. These places were famous for that. Fangs.

He shook through his pack to find an unsoaked smoke, which he then lit with his lighter, dangerous motion or not. The fatigue of prolonged tension had weakened his limbs and they began to shudder. His life was all a dream now back there behind his eyes and he thought of highlights from it when he had fun or fought and won. Then some when he lost. And other times, too, when he'd been up to this or that but all of them began to have an "Oh, shit, I never should've did that" coda tacked on.

They want me dead now. Stone cold and dirt hidden.

He flipped the cigarette butt away from himself in a loop and it disappeared instantly, not even the smoke of it left in the air.

Yeah — it's like that.

Pete Ledoux had managed to unjam the shotgun, and when he'd gone back to the house Peggy had uncovered the good paper shells, which made him want to finger God or something. So much of life had come to him that way, too late, overdue, never enough of it there when it did show up.

This whole thing was fucked up beyond taking pride in

167

now. You devise a scheme like an exotic domino loop but if the first bone tumbles sideways instead of straight it won't fall in the design you planned for. So then you made it up as you went. That meant trouble.

The Cobb kid had some kind of ridiculous gris-gris working for him, too. That couldn't've been planned for. You never know who'll have luck like that and certainly not why. Any grumbling about fairness was for kids and clergy.

Ledoux's face was pebbled with mosquito bites. Forget the Cutter's and that means every needle-nose bug in the woods spare-changes you for blood like cornerboy hustlers spotting a strung-out Kennedy trying to score on Seventh. Like you got plenty to give.

The water reflected moonlight in between trees. Ledoux cut the engine and now pulled the boat down the waterways by grabbing at the dome of branches and vines. It seemed that all the twigs had stickers and where there weren't stickers there were natural points. He could feel the blood beading on his hands.

There were things running through the trees. Scampering things that chattered and squatty bold things that he could feel looking back at him. There were rabbits that could swim out here. Flying squirrels. Bobcats that weren't too good at either feat but ended up eating plenty anyway. That seemed natural somehow.

None of this was new to him, not swampy nights or mortal chases or killing. He'd seen it all before. The sounds were not baffling nor were the sensations of the hunt. But when he did hear something that pricked his senses he knew it was a man. Then he knew the metallic click as that of a lighter being lit. Straining, it seemed that he could hear an inhalation, even the dull smoky taste, that was coming to him, too.

He was trying to scent in on the cigarette but that smoky

hint was hard to locate. Ledoux slid out of the boat and sank titty deep into the water. He held the shotgun level with his forehead and walked with the sluggish current at his back. That Zippo click clue seemed to have come from the peak of a mudbank that was covered by cockspur hawthorn.

Must be very careful and silent, get into range, then boom! boom! and birds and squirrels and even some unnameables will scatter like that peckerwood's head. To quieter places.

Even in daylight it was hard to tell solid ground from sinkhole in this place. Take a step wrong and you'll come up coughing shit that flushed out of St. Louis about a year ago. The surface of the water was coated with scum, branches, and greenery, looking like a path to morons. Like fool's gold, only it was earth. Fool's earth.

Ledoux walked down the slough, holding his upper body rigid, stepping stiff-legged underwater to avoid splashing. When his feet slipped he went with the slide instead of fighting it. The key to the swamp was to agree with it, accept the way it was.

As Ledoux worked his way toward the suspect mudbank he knew that this whole affair was too sloppy to come through unhurt. Bound to get caught out in a messy deal like this. He knew he could do another bit in Jeff City if he had to, not standing on his head or without taking his shoes off, but he could stand it. But he couldn't handle pulling life and that Cobb kid could whine some plea-bargain ballad that would get that done to him.

Plenty of reason to erase the boy's voice right there, even if he didn't, by now, just plain old *want* to kill him.

Everything was pale in the sky, black on the ground, gray in the nightwash that was the huge in between. Shade tried to will his eyes to adjust, to focus into X ray and show him where he was. He was as lost as any child could get but more worried by it. He looked this way and that, and saw all that could be expected. It wasn't enough.

He thought about climbing one of the hairy-barked trees that cowlicked out of sight. But it'd just be to rip his britches and see more trees and less ground. No point.

Shade had quit on trying to stay dry. Wetness was dues in a swamp, and he had paid up, first just to his knees, then a backstep misstep had put him into the thick water, flat, face up, nostril-deep. Unknown things rubbed against his skin and he had frequently walked into the ditch-spanning webs of absurdly ambitious spiders. They felt like nets breaking over his head and shoulders, sticking like spun sugar.

Leeches.

Shade's hands went inside his shirt. He ran his fingers over the tautness of his chest and belly, and found three moist clingers at his midriff. They felt like nose hockers but they'd buried their heads and wouldn't pull loose. Have to singe them out. Shade slumped. Forget them for now.

He trudged on resolutely, staying in the ditch water because once you were past dainty notions of dryness it was the clearest path to follow. The growth on the banks was an incestuous tangle of verdure. No single plant stood out, just a solid mass of related limbs and leaves and vines, all atop one another with stickers on the handholds.

The hum of everything that flowed or splashed, sang or chattered, was in constant need of deciphering. Was that a footstep? A cough? Wind? A rifle sighting in on the back of your head?

At some places the bottom went deep and Shade had to dog-paddle to the next muck promenade. He tried to keep his pistol dry but it didn't really matter.

After a while he began to hear a soft thump, a regular flat

tap that seemed out of rhythm. He went toward it but couldn't see what it was until he was nearly touching it.

A johnboat adrift. That meant two people at least were out there somewhere.

Shade chinned himself on the gunwale, tilting the boat for a look inside. Nothing but a cracked paddle and an empty coffee can. He'd thought there might be an inert someone in the boat and was not entirely relieved that there wasn't.

As he released the gunwale and eased back down into the water, he found himself remembering a time that he kept hoping he would forget. It had been one of those gentle summer nights when the whole world had sweet breath, especially if you were sixteen and barely scarred, and he'd felt magically carefree, standing as he was in front of De Geere's Skelly Station because it was the closest place to home that sold red cream soda, holding a handful of bottletops that he flying-saucered across the traffic. On such a night he had believed that no one could take offense at harmless fun, even if the serrated disks had skimmed the hood of your new Impala. So he had hardly noticed the car suddenly whipping to the curb and the wad of man that jumped onto the sidewalk before the door could bounce shut behind him. The man was thirtyish with high straight shoulders and a face that said he had many scores to settle but couldn't, yet had lucked onto one that he could. As he closed gregariously on teenaged Shade, his cheeks jerked and he said, "Don't mess with me. You're goin' to learn that."

Shade was surprised witless, an incredulous smile on his face, holding his soda and the remaining tops. "What's the problem?"

"Ain't none." And a serious fist popped upside Shade's head. He saw stars and daylight and fell, then skittered on his hands and knees across the pavement. A toe caught him in the

171

butt, hurting more than he thought it could. He came up then with the Big Boy cream soda bottle and whacked the man on the elbow, which straightened his arm, then on the ear, which downed him. Shade stood over the flat man and shook with indecision, then bent and bashed the prominent teeth out, then hit again in the empty spot, blood pulp and white chips flecking his hand.

Old lazy-eyed De Geere had come running from the limestone station, "Get on out of here!" Then, as Shade stood by dumbly, "See what you done? You done killed the man, fool! Whoever told you you was tough, you sissy? 'Cause you ought've done it to them! You just one more Frogtown idiot boy."

And for two wired, crazy days he had run for relatives, believing that it was true, he'd killed a man and life was over.

But he hadn't really, and it wasn't, but that is when it had started to change.

Not much for it but to sit it out, Jewel thought. Off to one side he could see a tree that was leafless, drowned by too much water. The tree rose all dead by itself amid the live ones, beckoning like a lean-fingered taunt from the deep-sixed beyond.

Why would one die from what the rest get fat on?

He was in contemplation of that and other big questions, like had his life turned in the fifth grade when he'd had a teacher he could tell to shove it and she'd just shrug, when he began to hear the sounds.

Somebody was coming up the little rise, not even being too quiet about it. Boots dragged in the mud and saplings were bent into grips. Loud breaths.

Running wasn't worth it anymore. After this there could be nowhere left to run. He was caught. There were men who'd been shot up to seventeen times and lived to talk about it too much, and commandos with shoe-polish faces could slit half a dozen sentry throats in a night's work. But he didn't have a blade or any real confidence that he was one of those seventeen-bullet guys.

So he sat back in the shadows and waited, wanting only to die like a man, although no one much would ever know if he did or he didn't. Not out here.

The noise was closer now, on top of the bank. He could see that it was Pete the frogfucker he never should've known.

He watched as Pete poised catlike and swiveled his eyes all around the dark spots and tangled shapes. There was nothing for it now, and Jewel's hand hoisted a chunk of rock. He stood, hoping only to bean the guy once before he was exploded across the woods like so much red sand.

"Yo, Pete," he called. "You wouldn't be lookin' for me, would you?"

Ledoux hunkered small at the jibe of the voice, his fingers tapping on the stock of the shotgun, his body swinging toward the sound.

"Hey, boy. Why'd you run out?"

Shade, immobilized by the memory of a man he'd almost killed, was shaken when he heard something a little bit clumsy going up a muddy incline straight ahead, rustling bushes. He crouched in the water and stared toward the sound. There was more of it. The mud terrace had cockspur all over it, and he distinctly heard a sharp breath. He began to slow-motion through the water, careful not to splash, sneaking up from behind.

Moonlight oozed through the trees and spotted the water now and then. In one such brief illumination Shade saw the surface wriggle with a chilling sashay two steps in front of him.

173

Cottonmouth.

He stood still but the snake had some interest in him and turned toward the heat of his body. The curiosity of the reptile had peril at its core, and Shade pulled no air, shyly watching the triangular head weave side to side to within inches of his face. He tried to not look edible and to remember correctly the folklore that said either snakes never bite in the water or they *only* bite when afloat. It was confused in his mind.

The snake's length was strung out in the weak current, but his head was still right there.

The sound on the mudbank became louder and regular, then there was a blast of a shotgun and a yell.

Shade cupped both hands beneath the water, then shoved a wave at the snake and dove to his right, his face submerging. When he came up he began to run toward the shot, looking for the cottonmouth that he couldn't see, reaching for his pistol which he pulled and cocked.

In the pause, Jewel heard the click of the safety being punched off. It rang out like half of a ding-dong.

"Couldn't stand the idea of corned beef, you frogfuckin' shit."

One of the myriad of shroud shadows moved and Ledoux stared at the area. He peered into the thicket, then shot, hoping for luck.

The pellets ripped through the leaves above Jewel, pattering like supercharged rain. He fell to the ground and began to crawl. His elbows squeaked in the mud. The rock was still in his hand, but useless.

Rapid splashes began to sound from the ditch down the mudbank. A pistol was fired in the air.

Jewel saw Ledoux stop, startled by the new dynamics, and

thought, Duncan, Duncan has come to the aid of blood thicker than any water, even this.

Quickly another form appeared and a voice unrelated to him said, "Don't, Ledoux!"

Ledoux backed toward Jewel, going "Huh?" then suddenly fired at the man. The pellets were screened by the curtain of leaves and limbs and the man did not fall or even cry out. He fired back, and Ledoux did a headfirst backflop into the mud, the shotgun flying from his hands.

Just one bullet, Jewel thought.

He went after the body with the rock swinging his hand, knowing that he didn't know much but this was it. No mistake.

One more chance.

Shade came forward under the trees, his pistol hand trembling, his gaze centered on the man he'd just tumbled. The man was bucking convulsively and groaning a long single tone.

The shooting had the sanctity of self-defense but the gurgle of the downed man ruled out any feeling of righteousness. Shade had never shot another man and he walked cautiously, looking for the shotgun that might still figure in all of this.

A wild screaming blond came running from the dark, crouched to the ground, one hand raised above his head.

"Stop!" Shade yelled.

But the blond closed on Ledoux and began to beat at the fallen man with a frenzy of blows. Something cracked and the feral sounds from both men were raised in a sickening duet.

"Damn it, stop!"

Shade stepped quickly to the men and shoved Cobb away. He saw the rock in the boy's hand and pointed his pistol in his face.

"No more, Cobb."

Jewel breathed loudly, sitting back on his haunches, his legs spread before him.

"I got to kill him, he wants to kill me." Jewel sucked for air and jerked his words. "He wants to kill me." He looked up at Shade, his eyes glowing. "I'm a killer."

"No, it's over. It's over."

Jewel backed off and lay on the ground, sobbing for breath.

Kneeling, Shade checked Ledoux. He'd been ripped in the lower left chest, inches below the heart. Blood was leaping from the wound. Cobb's rock pummeling appeared to have been ineffective, only adding some deep bruises to his chest.

"It's bad," Ledoux said. "I know. Oh, shit this upstream life."

Shade stiffened his fingers straight, then pressed them inside the hot wound, trying to block the hole.

"Oh! Oh!"

"You try to run, Cobb, and I'll kill you."

"I guess I won't," Jewel said, his voice dreamy with weakness.

"We can't get out of here in the dark, Ledoux," Shade said. He pressed his fingers against the moist rim of the wound he'd given the man. "You'll have to hang on."

They all sat silently for a moment. Ledoux, his face warping with pain, stared up at Shade.

"I've seen you," he said.

"I'm Rene Shade. I want you to know."

"Ugh. Sure. Lafitte Street Shades. Shot by you."

"You made me."

"Oh, I remember you, mon petit homme. You ain't clean. None of you are."

Shade nodded.

"You were a punk," Ledoux said, his voice warbling, his breath flecking blood. "You stole, all of you."

"Yes."

"Oh, hell, you've shot me. *You*."

The sounds of the swamp had come back to life, the intrusion of the shots having been forgotten. The amphibian blats and limb-rattling movements of coons and others sounded all around.

"You hurt people," Ledoux said. "Where do you get off shootin' me?"

"I never would've killed," Shade said. "Take it easy, Ledoux. You would've."

"So? Ugh, ugh. I had ambitions, so?"

"Save your strength."

Jewel Cobb was now relaxed with the final relief of having been caught. He lay on his belly, head on arms, and mumbled sleepily into the mud. Shudders made his body palpitate in the muck, and his voice would raise incoherently.

For a long time Shade had hopes that Ledoux would live, but he felt the odds get longer against that chance with each squirt through his fingers.

Once Ledoux raised his head, with an effort that shocked by its difficulty, and said, "Can I be forgiven?"

"I don't know."

Ledoux slumped back.

"Fuck it."

"Maybe."

Soon after that Shade withdrew his fingers from their pointless position and leaned against a tree trunk, weary, sick to the bone, and sad. He looked up through the trees where a bit of sky showed. Since the swamp was essentially impenetrable at night, they could not leave until morning and help arrived. He sat looking at the sky and the corpse he'd made, waiting.

Waiting.

As the night sky began to pale, carp, following some primal

urge, came up to the mudbanks and began their fishy barks that sounded the coming of dawn. The weird prehistoric grunts roused Shade from a flinching slumber.

The Cobb kid was still asleep and the world was coming awake. The sun rose pink in the east and the various flows seemed somehow louder in the light.

Shade, his eyes like robin's eggs in tablespoons of blood, stood when full dawn arrived. Soon he heard them. The full throttle hum of searching boats.

He raised his pistol with a slack arm and fired the three SOS shots of one in distress, into the sinkhole tangle of the Marais du Croche.

THE COMING
DAYS

The heat hung around until it was no longer mentioned as weather but only as some cosmic revenge. The big brown garbage scow of a river began to steam with malodorous ferment, and one Nelda Lomeli, who had just the week before dredged out a channel cat with whiskers that would shame a weeping willow, and that dressed out to a grand eighty-four shit-fattened pounds, returned to the same spot. She cast into the water and when she began to reel in, found that she was snagged. Then she thought that perhaps it was another monster cat, and pulled hand over hand on the thick-twine line. Whatever it was lifted off the bottom and rode with the current and she stepped into the flow to grapple with it. She did not scream when the head and shoulders appeared, for she was a longtime river woman, but she didn't want to touch it.

Finally she dragged the bloated body to the lip of the sandbar, and Duncan Cobb, with a whole lot of extra mouth where his throat used to be, was found.

Alvin Rankin was now dead to the withered-wreath stage, and downtown, in the white stone City Hall, Eddie Barclay, a terra-cotta runner-up, was sworn in as his replacement. Mayor Crawford proclaimed it a continuation of Rankin's good work, and Barclay, as his first official act, gave the Music Center contract to Dineen Construction of Hawthorne Hills and was instantly free of debt.

Over where the windows had bars and shoestrings were considered to be a temptation to take the easy way out, Jewel Cobb sat awaiting trial. He knew nothing, everyone he could finger was dead, and his ignorance was so convincing and total that he had little to bargain with. So he was pleaded guilty but not special, although he knew that a jury of his peers, even selected by the random dozen, would recognize the punch line way before the end of *that* joke.

And the baffling events of summer had another daffy moment when Steve Roque carried his trash to the curbside bins but found the twist tops of the garbage bags to be undone and paused to tie them, only to be shot for it under the arm, in the side, and just above the knee by some invisibles, who remained so. He would live, but never talk, and it was considered to be injury by misadventure.

But the town went on, Saint Bruno sucked up and staggered tall, for there were regular worries more pressing—like the floods that would come as they always had, and those pushed out by the rising tide would once more be driven before it, forced to connive toward all those higher grounds . . .

On a Sunday of continuing punishment, Rene Shade, out for a peaceful drive, passed the Catfish Bar and saw his brother in the doorway. He pulled into the lot and let himself in. Tip was sweeping the floor, all alone.

"I've been wanting to see you," Shade said.

Tip paused with the broom in his hand, then dropped it.

"You've had plenty of time. Haven't seen you in weeks. I've been expectin' you."

"Fix me a drink."

"Why not."

When Tip went behind the bar, Shade followed. He leaned against the cooler and watched Tip lift a bottle of rum.

"I had to kill a man because you lied to me, Tip."

"Don't lay that off on me, li'l blood. That's your job. You picked it."

"Cobb was right there in your kitchen and you didn't tell me."

Tip scooted the rum along the bar.

"I didn't really know what was goin' on, man."

"You could be busted for that."

"Bullshit. It'd never stick and you know it. How's your drink?"

"I'm very angry."

"Nothin' you can do about it. Now drink your drink and get —"

Shade's right hand banged the heavy whiskey glass on his brother's jaw. The big man was stunned but managed to throw a windy left that spun him when it missed, and Shade stepped in with a pop to the mouth and a quick knee to the groin. As Tip began to slide down Shade dropped the glass, then threw an overhand right at his dodgeless brother, and knocked him cold.

He stood there over the sack of flesh that was related to him in too many ways and began to shake. Blood was flooding from his brother's mouth and his eyeballs shuddered behind their lids.

He shoved open the cooler and grabbed a handful of ice, then knelt to Tip. He cradled his head in his lap and held the ice to the torn mouth.

"You dumb bastard," he said, his eyes blinking rapidly, "I love you."